THE ALIEN'S BATTLE

OUTCASTS OF CORIN

ELLA MAVEN

ONE

Trix

Without my weapons, I felt helpless. I hadn't realized how much I relied on my collection of blades and arrows until they were stripped from me.

I huddled in the center of the cage and glared at any of the red aliens who came close. I'd thought I'd seen ugly aliens, but they didn't come close to these guys—the Joktal. Red-skinned like the devil, four-armed, and massive, their heads were a mass of thick bone shaped like an upside-down triangle with horns wider than their shoulders curving out from the top two points.

They didn't really have lips—more of a gaping maw with sharp teeth and a flat face except for bulging oval eyes. The one who walked alongside my wheeled cage held the leash of an eye-less hunch-backed hound with one of his lower arms. With a bony-plated upper arm, he reached out and rattled my cage. Just for fun. Because they were dicks.

I didn't react. The last time I'd yelled at them, they'd

laughed and mocked me while cracking their glowing whips near the bars of my cage. At the thought of one of those touching my skin, I broke out in a cold sweat.

I missed my friends. Their absence was worse than a limb amputation. There were only seven of us, but we'd bonded over the unspeakable horrors we'd been put through since the day we woke up on a spaceship rocketing from Earth. We'd escaped our captors and had tried to make a life for ourselves as nomads on this planet until our camp was invaded by massive bipedal warthogs who smelled like rotten meat.

I could still hear the anguish in Tasha's voice as she'd called my name. I hadn't been able to respond as the pain of the warthog's grip had stolen my breath. And that was a lingering regret—that I hadn't responded. That I hadn't tried harder. That I'd failed.

Dropping my forehead onto my folded arms, I clenched my jaw as I willed the tears to remain at bay. I wouldn't cry. I had to remain strong. I'd been delivered to these red aliens by the warthog fuckers, and they hadn't killed me yet, which had to mean something. Instead, we'd been traveling for days through dense jungle growth, over open fields, and across rivers. Their hounds pulled my cage with thick chains attached to their harnesses. At the beginning, I'd been motion sick from the rocking of the cage on the uneven ground, but I must have gotten sea-legs... er, cage-legs... and now could keep down the meager rations they supplied me.

I'd tried to ask where they'd taken my friends—the other human females—and they'd ignored me. I couldn't imagine how scared Lu and Maisie were. They had always been the most emotionally fragile. Tasha would feel guilty, Amber would be vulnerable because of her mod, and Neve... I wasn't sure how she would be coping.

I had held it together so far... as long as they didn't touch me. I'd always viewed my weapons as an offensive strategy, but now I realized I'd very much relied on them as defensive protection.

Through the trees, the dark form of a structure began to take shape. I uncurled from my hunched position and crawled to the side of my cage. The Joktals ignored me, as their pace seemed to speed up, and within minutes, the trees cleared to reveal a massive fortress with walls easily two-to-three stories high.

Two large, gated doors opened as the cage wheels rattled onto a wooden plank path leading inside. I swallowed down the bile threatening to rise in my throat. My brain screamed at me that entering those walls would mean nothing good, but I didn't have a choice. Locked in a cage, surrounded by massive aliens and their sharp-fanged hounds, I could do nothing but sit in terror as we entered the gates.

Inside, the cage rattled to a stop and the hounds who'd been pulling me pawed at the dirt of a barren courtyard. An unusual structure stood along one wall—a tall pillar with chains dangling from it. Each ended with a manacle. I shuddered and looked away.

Before me were several structures, a few buildings, and one massive tower taller than the fortress walls.

From the base of the tower, a group of half a dozen Joktals emerged. I studied them as they drew closer. The one walking in front wore a vest adorned with studs along with a belt strapped to his massive girth. From it hung several blades and one of those glowing whips. The other Joktals were not as armed and each wore nothing but pants, boots, and a simple sash. The Joktals around me—I'd arrived in a fleet of a dozen—stood with their lower arms clasped behind their backs and their upper arms loose at their sides.

He reached my cage and stopped a few feet away. Head cocked, he peered between the bars at me like I was a bug to be studied. I resisted the urge to spit at him.

"Bring her out," he barked.

I was grateful that they'd updated my translation implant with their language, so at least I wasn't in the dark when they spoke. The fleet I'd traveled with rarely spoke, and I was sure that was on purpose, so I'd have as little information as possible. They'd only spoken to me when they gave me orders.

A Joktal opened my cage and reached inside to drag me out. I scrambled away from him, launching myself out of the cage into the dirt and immediately rising on my own. They thought I just despised their touch, which was correct, but they didn't know that even the most minor of grips caused me immeasurable pain. I planned to hide that as long as possible, so they didn't use my weakness against me.

My eyes darted around me as my instincts told me to run. Of course, that would be stupid and get me nowhere. The hounds would be on me before I could take two strides, but I couldn't help the urge to flee now that I was finally uncaged.

"I wouldn't advise running, human," the vested Joktal said. "You won't get far."

I didn't respond as I clenched my fists at my sides and told myself to be smart. Stay calm. Get information.

"I'm Upreth Hangrin, commander of the Joktal kerth and Joktalis," he said, and I didn't miss the way his chest puffed out. Like I was supposed to be impressed. He gestured with his lower arms at the surrounding fortress.

They'd named their city after themselves. Why did that not surprise me?

He stared at me expectantly, as if I was supposed to respond. What did he want me to say? Congratulations?

When I didn't answer, his bulging eyes narrowed, and he turned to the guard near my cage. "Can she talk? I was told her language has been identified and my implant was updated."

"She does speak, commander," the guard answered. "Mostly insults."

"Oh, fuck off, asshole," I muttered.

The guard tilted his head at me as if to say, *See?*

Upreth flicked his fingers at another guard, who stepped forward with a large sack. He dumped the contents into the dirt, and I held back a gasp as my handmade bow, arrows, and several blades clattered to the ground. I'd thought they were gone forever.

"Her weapons. She was the warrior of the band of females."

That was stretching it a bit, but I'd take it.

Upreth picked up one of my crude blades. "Not much of a warrior since she's been caged and lost her females."

I felt my lips pulled back into a snarl. "Fuck—"

"She wounded one of the Wutarks commander," the guard cut me off. "She should be considered dangerous."

It was my turn to puff my chest out. I shot the commander a smug look, which he absolutely did not appreciate as he took a step forward and backhanded me with one of his bony plates.

The world tipped as pain exploded in my face and echoed throughout my entire body. I hit the dirt in a boneless heap and gasped for air. My head swam, my vision blurred, and I fought to remain conscious.

"Without her weapons, she's a declawed and defanged salibri." The commander's voice sounded underwater.

I shook my head and tried to focus.

"Harmless," he spat.

I had to get to my feet. I couldn't let him stand over me like this. It took a gargantuan effort to gather my legs under me and rise. For a moment, I saw two commanders until my vision finally settled and he morphed into one vicious asshole.

"Pick on..." I rasped. "Someone your own size."

He let out a bellow that sounded somewhere between a parrot caw and a hyena cackle. The sound sent a tremor down my spine, but I held my ground.

"I'm sorry for the disruption of your home. We made... a mistake."

I blinked. "A mistake?"

"You fought for your friends. You want them found and unharmed, yes?"

My pain took a backseat as I latched onto his words like a lifeline. "Where are they? Where did the Wutarks take them?"

Upreth's evil eyes gleamed. "They were stolen from the Wutarks by a clavas of nasty species called the Drixonians. Unfortunately, the Drixonians will use them to breed more of their kind."

My voice went hoarse as my stomach dropped to my feet. "Breed?"

"But you can help."

My head spun, but it wasn't from the pain. All I could think about was my precious Lu and my brave Tasha violated by massive brutes. "I'm going to be sick," I mumbled.

"You will be the bait we need to capture their leader.

Once we have him, we can use him to defeat his clavas and free your friends. And then we'll leave you humans alone. You won't see us again."

"How do I know you're telling the truth?" I asked.

He snapped his fingers and a Joktal behind him handed him a tablet. He tapped the screen and then turned it to me. For a moment, I couldn't make out what I was seeing, but then I focused on the colorized grainy image. A large alien with blue and black mottled skin, a tail, and horns was in mid-stride beneath a tree. Draped over his back was a human form. I couldn't see her face, but the hair... the hair I'd recognized anywhere. Long, curly, and golden. *Amber.*

I gasped and took a faltering step back. Losing my balance, I went to one knee. She'd been taken by an alien who planned to breed her. My sweet, quiet Amber. My heart pounded and my stomach protested my last meal. I just barely managed not to vomit.

"This is the only image we caught of them, but we have learned they have the rest of your females."

I glanced up. "All of them?"

He nodded. I wasn't sure he was telling the truth, but it didn't really matter. Even if only Amber was in the clutches of these aliens, I had to do everything I could to free her.

I slowly stood and forced myself to remain in control when all I wanted to do was rage and scream and cry. "You need me to act as bait to catch the leader?"

"Yes. Once he sees you, he will do all he can to acquire you. Human females are of great desire to them."

Gross. I straightened my back. "I'll do it."

Upreth grinned. At least, I was pretty sure it was a grin, even though he had no lips, but his eyes seemed to crinkle at the corners and let out another delighted cackle sound. "I knew you'd agree. The rumors about humans being stupid aren't true."

I wanted to tell him to take his rumors and shove them up his ass. "How soon can we go?"

Upreth's lower hands stroked the coiled whip at his belt. His tongue snaked out to run along the sharp edges of his teeth. "Now."

Now ended up being after a meal. I wasn't hungry but ate anyway. Most of the gathered Joktals sat on the ground in the courtyard, shoving disks of hard bread with dried meats into their faces. After being cramped inside the cage for so long, I stood to eat under the watch of a few guards.

Upreth walked around as if rallying his troops. I didn't understand what he'd meant about capturing us as a mistake. How had that been a mistake? I didn't believe that. Maybe all along he'd planned to capture us and use us as bait for these Drixonians. Whatever, it didn't matter. All that mattered now was getting my girls back. And then... well, depending on their condition, I'd decide if I needed to exact some revenge on the Joktal's. Humans *weren't* stupid, especially us, who had lived through what felt like several lifetimes.

After our meal, they fortunately did not shove me back behind bars. My cage was invisible now, as it was the promise that I'd see my friends again.

"The leader of the clavas is on his way back from their home city," Upreth said as we walked through dense brush. "We're not prepared to take on the entire Drixonian population, but we've identified this clavas as isolated."

That made sense. "So, what do I have to do?"

"We cannot cross the borders in large numbers, not enough to bring down a Drixonian leader. But you can position yourself on his homeward path." He handed me my bow and one of my arrows. "Shoot him with this. Nowhere fatal. We want him alive. The tip is poisoned with an herb that will render him unconscious." Next, he handed me a small cylinder. "Then send this signal into the air. We will send a few Joktals over the border and drag him back."

I took the items, noting the arrow point glistening with poisoned oil. My hands shook slightly, and I did my best to hide that from Upreth. I wasn't worried about harming this Drixonian. I would have killed him if they asked me too in order to free my girls. I was concerned I'd mess this up. My friends' safety rode on my shoulders.

When we reached the borders, Upreth gave me explicit instructions on how to travel the rest of the way to cross the Drixonian's path. I ventured a few paces away and looked over my shoulder. Upreth remained where he stood, a dozen guards at his back. He motioned with all four arms for me to keep going.

I took a few more careful steps as I kept a large tree in the distance in my sightline. Upreth said as long as I kept that in front of me, I'd encounter the Drixonian. Soon, I could no longer see the Joktals, and unease slithered under my skin. Should I run? They'd left me unattended. But then, how would I ever find Amber and the rest of my girls? I hated that I couldn't trust the Joktals, and that I didn't know their motive other than to capture this Drixonian.

Legs aching and sweat dripping down my back, I walked for what felt like an hour. Maybe it was a half hour. Maybe it was more. I couldn't tell, and it seemed like the sun had moved little. I traveled over some fields of yellow flowers and in the distance, I swore I could hear the rush of water.

Suddenly, a new sound floated on the breeze. I froze for a moment before sprinting the rest of the way across the field and diving behind a tree. The buzzing sound grew louder until movement in the trees caught my attention. A large black wheel-less motorcycle skirted the edge of the field and perched on top like some sort of alien biker was a massive blue and black alien.

Sharp black horns corkscrewed out of the side of his head, and a pelt of fur lay draped on his broad shoulders. Instead of eyebrows, a row of bumps highlighted his prominent brow. Studded with bladed armor, his tail whipped in the air behind him. Long, dark hair swirled around his head and his violet eyes glowed fiercely.

I'd seen one of these aliens before, briefly and from a distance. This close, I was struck a little dumb by his intimidating energy. I was supposed to shoot this guy?

I took a step out from behind the tree, and I knew the second he spotted me. His head jerked up, his eyes settled on me like laser, and he banked the bike, which hovered a few feet in the air thanks to the powerful jets of air underneath.

He leaped off the bike before it settled on the ground, landing in a neat crouch. When he rose to his full height, I noticed he had a long sword strapped to his back with a leather harness.

Fuck, he was huge, and *scary*. He watched me like a hawk watched its prey, and he walked with a predator's careful, graceful steps. The Joktals had been right. I was a *prize* for this Drixonian. He wanted me. How had Amber felt when one of these brutes grabbed her? Was it this one? Or another one? I'd vowed I'd never be owned by anything ever again, and I had also vowed to protect my friends from the same fate. But this blue alien had now threatened that. *Fuck them.*

He said something in a guttural language I didn't understand. The Joktals didn't deem it necessary for me to understand him. My bow and arrow remained strapped to my back, hidden from view. I just need him to come a little closer, so he was within my range. He spoke again, and his time he seemed angry. Did he expect me to come to him like a good little breeder? My lips peeled back from my teeth.

In about five more feet, he'd be close enough to shoot. "Come on," I whispered, and his gaze dropped to my mouth. I felt a flush of heat at the way his eyes fired. He came to a halt, and I nearly groaned because he was still out of range. His nostrils flared, and his hands flexed.

Shit, what if he had a laser gun? Something to incapacitate *me*? I had to act now. *Offense. Offense.*

With a cry, I lunged forward while reaching behind my back for the bow and arrow. I notched it on the run, and the Drixonian's eyes went wide. He bellowed out a word, but I'd already let the arrow fly. The tip pierced his shoulder, and his body jerked at the impact, but he didn't fall. His gaze dropped to the arrow sticking out of his arm. As he yanked it out easily, black blood oozed down his arm. His fingers tapped up the shaft until he reached the end where I'd carved a maple leaf into the wood.

His eyes flicked to me as he tossed the arrow to the ground and walked forward, faster this time. My breath caught. Why wasn't he going down? He needed to pass out. *Now.*

Panic flared in my chest as I stumbled backward. "Stop," I called out, as if that would do anything, but this wasn't going the way it was supposed to. The Drixonian was still moving, still advancing...

Suddenly his steps faltered, and his arms flung out at the sides as if to keep his balance. He shook his head and took another step forward, but his leg buckled, and he went down on one knee.

I nearly wept with relief when his body listed to the side. That was when his head lolled, and he speared me with one last purple gaze. And what I saw there wasn't what I'd expected. He looked... betrayed. In the next second, his body pitched over with a thump in the long grass.

I hit the dirt on my knees, slammed the flare against my thigh, and stared as the red spark bolted high into the sky.

TWO

KUTZAL

My head ached, like I'd gone on a bender with too many spirits back at camp. I opened my eyes, but that action alone took more effort than it should have. I stared up at metal bars, which were a little too close for my liking, and rolled my head to the side to see vegetation beyond more bars. Briggers chirped somewhere overhead, and footsteps whispered through the grass. I caught sight of a few trees.

Where the hell was I?

I tried to sit up, but my stomach protested, and I bit back a groan. I had to take one thing at a time. I wiggled my toes in my boots, moved my legs and then my arms. I was alive and apparently had all my limbs. A dull ache in my shoulder drew my attention, and my left arm was crusted with blood.

Then it came back to me. The female with dark red hair. Green eyes. Slender build. She'd shot me with a flecking arrow. I'd tried to walk toward her and then everything went hazy. The arrow tip must have been spiked with something.

When I'd pulled it out of my shoulder, I'd known immediately that she was a friend of Amber and Tasha's, the mates to my warriors Vinz and Lukent, because those females had shown me the arrow with the five-pointed leaf and identified it as belonging to their friend. Her name was... ah, I couldn't remember. My mind was working a little slow.

I rolled my head to the side, wondering if I was going to find myself captured by a roving band of human females, which might have been a Drixonian dream but was actually *my* nightmare. But there I did not immediately see any human females. Attached to chains which pulled my cage on its wheels were hairy eye-less hounds that trotted with hunched backs. And peering into my cage with a delighted sneer on his ugly face... was a Joktal.

At least, I was pretty sure it was a Joktal with his four-arms, triangle head, and flat face. That checked out with the description Vinz had used. He'd been captured by these fleckers too, and then he'd escaped with his human mate.

Speaking of... where was that flecking female who'd shot me? They must have captured her too. I sat up, expecting to find another cage with the female inside, but found her perfectly alive, well, and *free*. She walked near my cage of her own volition, appearing perfectly safe and unharmed.

I growled low in my throat. Had she helped these fleckers? This was why I didn't like anyone other than Drixonians. I couldn't trust them, even human females. I would do everything I could to protect females—*She is All*, after all— but I didn't have to *like* them.

Suddenly, the female's head swung to face me, and her

eyes met mine. She didn't appear remorseful as her jaw clenched, and she sent me a nasty glare.

"You're making a big mistake, female," I growled at her.

She didn't respond at all. A Joktal slapped the cage with a bony-plated arm. "She can't understand you, Drix. Don't bother."

"It doesn't matter," she snapped. I could see the implant behind her ear and assumed she knew the Joktals' language, but not mine. I could understand her as my implant had been updated so I could converse with the Drixonian's human mates. She turned a vicious glare on me that might have felled some of the younger Drix warriors. "I know all about how you stole my friends to breed them. Rapist fucks."

My cora twisted painfully in my chest at her words. I spun in a circle in my cage, which was surrounded by about a dozen Joktals. "Is that what you told her?" I roared at anyone and everyone. "That we breed females *against their will?*"

The cage rattled to a stop, and momentum slid me forward until I slammed into the front bars of the cage. But I didn't even register the pain as my body flared with undiluted anger.

The Joktals in front of my cage parted, and a Joktal with an adorned vest stepped forward. He was clearly some sort of leader, and I tried to straighten with as much dignity as I could muster in the cage.

"You are Kutzal Bane, drexel of the Lone Howl Drixonian clavas," he said.

Seeing as I wasn't impressed that he knew my identity, I remained silent. He huffed, as if annoyed I didn't give a shet.

He puffed out his chest. "I'm Upreth, commander of Joktalis."

"Great. Introductions done," I said in a monotone. "Now what the fleck am I in this cage for?"

A guard nearby reached through the bars and cuffed me on the head. "Show some respect."

"Fleck off," I spat at him.

"He seems to have learned his communication skills the same place the female has," Upreth inhaled sharply through his nose holes.

I wasn't sure what that meant, so I didn't answer. They'd taken my weapons and my tail armor. Behind these bars, my machets were useless. If only I could get out of this cage, I'd lay waste to these fleckers. The most important thing they'd taken? The translation implant updater I'd had on me. If only I could get that back and converse with this female, I could convince her to free me. She *owed* me seeing as I had helped keep her friends safe. Once I got my hands on this female... well, I wouldn't hurt her. But she'd get the sharp side of my tongue. Tasha and Amber thought I was a mean fleck? At least they hadn't shot me with a poisoned arrow.

She caught me glaring at her and lifted her hand in the air with her middle finger extended. I had no idea what that meant, but I did it back anyway. Her eyes registered surprise, and I swore I saw the beginning of a smile before she coughed into her hand and turned away.

Upreth drew my attention when he huffed out a snort. "We're taking you to your camp, where we'll use you to acquire the surrender of your clavas."

I barked out a laugh. "Is that so? And what do you plan to do with my clavas after we surrender?"

His eyes gleamed. "Eradicate you."

My heart pounded, and my vision went white at the edges as I fought to keep from beating against the bars of the cage like a barbarian. "You can try," I snarled.

"And I promised this human that we'd free her friends from their Drixonian oppressors, didn't I?"

The red-haired female stared back at Upreth with undisguised disgust. "And you better hold up your end of the deal."

So, she didn't fully trust him either. A seed of hope sprouted in my chest.

"We will," he answered before turning to me. "One by one, we'll pick off every clavas until Granit is isolated and vulnerable. We have no desire to share this planet with you, and we don't intend to."

I had been content to respect borders as Dazeem Bakut, the head drexel of the remaining Drixonian clavases, had insisted on in order to keep the peace. We'd stay on our land, and they'd stay on theirs. It was a big planet. But now? Fleck them all. They'd kidnapped me, they'd lied to this female, and they intended to kill my warriors using me as leverage. I'd *eradicate* myself before they used me against my own warriors.

The only reason I hadn't sliced my throat with my own machets yet was because I couldn't be sure what they'd do to this female. Once they didn't have use for her, they would likely kill her. Free her friends? No way. They'd used her friend Amber as labor in Joktalis before she and Vinz escaped. Now they were a happily mated pair. If only this female knew how well her friends were cared for by their mates.

I stared back at Upreth, who watched me expectantly, clearly wanting a rise out of me. But I'd given them enough reactions for the day. I couldn't let my emotions get the best of me. From now on, I had to be level-headed and smart. So much was riding on me. As much as I trusted my warriors not to surrender to save my life, I couldn't be sure that Vinz wouldn't do something stupid, or Axton wouldn't risk it all for me.

So, I stared back at Upreth, refusing to give him the reaction he so clearly wanted.

With a sneer on his lipless mouth, he turned and marched forward. I watched his back until the guards closed ranks behind him. My cage rattled once again as the hounds pulling it began to walk. I sat down in the center of the cage, braced my wrists on my bent knees, and closed my eyes. I'd been in worse situations.

Back when the prospering Drixonian civilization ran this planet, the females of our species ruled our councils while the males were warriors whose job it was to defend. Every male was required to train at an early age and serve until they could retire. Desertion was the ultimate taboo, and when a warrior fled his duties, his entire family suffered. I was one of those sons whose father abandoned his post. Deemed a son of naught, I was branded on the back of my neck and shunned along with others like me.

But then a virus struck our civilization, killing all our females and most of our elder males. Heartbroken, devastated, and surrounded by a crumbling society, we left to join the Uldani on our sister planet, Torin. As sons of naught, we received the worst jobs for the Uldani, and some of us put through unspeakable horrors... like Vinz.

We didn't learn for many cycles that the Uldani were responsible for starting the virus in an effort to gain Drixonian warriors as soldiers. We rose up, gained our independence, and returned to our home planet, Corin. But it was different from how we left it. While Daz had relaxed the rules around the sons of naught and had no issue with our mating, I still felt fiercely protective of them. We'd come a long way since those shunned young Drix. I'd never let us be treated like dirt again.

No matter how much was stacked against me, I would win this battle.

Trix

They hadn't fed him, and that shouldn't have bothered me. But it did. The sun had set, and we'd stopped our progress for the night. The guards and Upreth sat around a crackling fire, ignoring the Drixonian prisoner. Upreth had said his name—Kutzal. Kutzal Bane. I hadn't really wanted to know his name, because that made it even more real that I'd taken part in the capture of a being with a name and a family and a soul.

But his soul was rotten, according to Upreth. And I had to believe that. I wanted to believe that. Because if that was wrong... Well, then what had I done?

I sat away from the fire, not eager to converse with the Joktal guards. While the cage had been cramped for me, this Drixonian was easily close to seven feet and couldn't even sit up straight. His shoulder and arm where I'd shot him remained covered in dried black blood, but he didn't seem bothered by the injury, which had already begun to close.

He had a long tail—thick at the base and then tapering into a narrow tip. His pants were held up with a type of backwards belt which clasped above the base of his tail. He no longer wore his harness of weapons, as they'd been stripped of him before they'd thrown his unconscious body in the cage. I did, however, make note of where they were—hidden in a sack carried by a guard. There'd been a few gadgets on his harness as well, which interested me.

In fact, the Drixonian himself interested me. I wasn't sure why. Upreth had told me he and his kind were a threat to my friends, but something about the way he looked at me was not congruent with how Upreth made them out to be. There was a high-level intelligence behind those purple eyes, even when he was angry. But ever since Upreth told him he planned to eradicate the Drixonians, Kutzal had fallen silent, contemplative. I sensed a simmering tension under his skin, but other than his initial outburst when he woke, he maintained control over his emotions in a way that impressed me.

He exuded an aura of pride, but not boastfulness like Upreth. There was a distinct difference between the way Kutzal possessed a powerful confidence and how Upreth wore the same, like an ill-fitting coat. I liked to think I was a good judge of character, but without being able to converse with Kutzal, I was only left with my gut feeling. Without my girls, I'd lost my footing a bit, and I couldn't be sure if I could trust my instincts. Since they were all I had, I knew I needed to get my head right. And soon.

I ate the bland meal bar and washed it down with some water. I had more left in my skin, and I knew every morning our skins would be refilled. I could drink more—which I didn't need—I could pour it out, or I could... share it with the Drixonian.

"Shit, Trix," I mumbled to myself. Why was I doing this? Why was I drawn to this blue alien? It wasn't like I had ever been into bad boys. I didn't write letters to inmates.

Back on Earth, I'd been an average kick boxing instructor with a pathetic social life.

When the Joktals began to bed down for the night, I remained sitting against the trunk of a tree, hidden in shadows. Upreth was the first one to sleep, and his snores filled the small clearing. A few guards stood watch, but they weren't paying any attention to me or to the Drixonian prisoner for that matter. They were stationed on the outskirts of the camp in case of intruders.

I couldn't tell if the Drixonian was awake or asleep as I inched closer to his cage on a low crouch. He sat propped up against the corner of the cage with one leg stretched out and the other bent at the knee. His tail, which seemed to be in constant motion, lay still.

The dying fire still offered enough light for me to see him better as I stopped outside his cage. The black and blue of his scales were blotchy like snakeskin and dulled to a lighter blue on the thinner skin of his face. One side of his long dark hair was tucked behind an ear studded with multiple golden piercings all along the rim which glittered in the firelight.

His black horns on either side of his head tapered to a sharp point that I imagined could do some real damage in battle. Eyes closed, his chest rose and fell with deep, even breaths.

The hand closest to me rested palm down on the bottom of the cage, and I noted the massive size. He could palm my head with that thing. Probably squish my skull and pop it like a grape. Not to mention his muscled chest and thick thighs... this alien was built like a brick shithouse.

Curious what his scales felt like, I reached through the bars of the cage and gently brushed my fingers along the skin of his wrist. The pads of my fingers burned slightly at the touch. His skin rippled, and then from beneath his scales, all along the outside of his forearm, a row of black blades emerged. I yanked my hand back, but I wasn't fast enough. Quick as lightning, his eyes popped open, purple irises glowing in the dark, and he grabbed my wrist. Pain shot up my arm as his skin came into contact with mine in a punishing grip. In order not to alert the guards, I clapped my hand over my mouth, but my knees buckled, and I knew my expression showed anguish.

As quick as he'd grabbed me, he let go as if electrocuted. I clutched my arm to my chest as the pain faded as quickly as it had come. The Drixonian was now on his knees at the edge of the cage, his fingers wrapped around the bars, and he stared down at me in what I could only see as... concern.

His chest heaved. "Guino," he said in a low rasp. "Beip gwenopha?"

Was he asking me if I was okay? Maybe he was trying to gain my trust, but I couldn't help but feel like he was genuinely concerned. He could tell I was in pain, and he didn't like it or want to be the cause of it. I felt that in my gut.

I rose to my feet. "I'm okay."

He relaxed slightly and sat back on his haunches. His gaze held mine until I squirmed and that was when I unhooked my water skin from my belt and held it through the bars of the cage. "Here's some water."

He didn't take it at first, and he looked at it suspiciously. He had every right since I *did* shoot him with a poisoned arrow. "I promise I didn't poison it."

The corners of his lips twitched as he snatched it and upended the entire thing in his mouth. A few drops escaped to slide down his thick neck and muscled pectorals. I caught myself chasing the beads of water as they slid over his abdomen and then down to the waistband of his pants. Instead of wiping his mouth, he snaked his tongue out to catch a few drops on his chin. Yes, his *chin*, because his tongue was like something out of a movie—long and thick, it stretched under his chin. In the center of this inhuman tongue were three golden ball piercings. My mouth went dry.

I shook myself out of my stupor to find him handing the skin back to me. He must have seen me ogling him, but he didn't leer, or smirk, or make any sort of reaction that I'd expect a male to make. His expression remained wary but not hostile.

My gut twisted. Had I made a mistake? But I couldn't get the picture out of my head of that blue warrior carrying Amber on his shoulder.

"My name is Trix." I chewed the inside of my cheek. "Do you know a human named Amber?"

He surged forward to grip the bars of his cage and his eyes held mine like a magnet. He opened his mouth, but before he could respond, his head whipped to the side. His rattling growl left his throat seconds before pain exploded in the back of my skull. Somewhere above me came a pained grunt just as my hip slammed into the ground so hard that my teeth clacked together.

I cried out as another blow hit me in the ribs. Lashing out with my legs, my foot connected with something, and a Joktal bellow followed.

No more blows came, and I stumbled to my feet, hands in front of me, ready to fight if I had to, but the Joktal guard who stood before me remained still with his bony upper arms lowered.

"What are you doing with the prisoner?" he snarled.

I tried to remember the names of the guards, but most of

them looked too much alike to tell apart. This one had a scar on his chest though. Yirij. That was his name.

"I just wanted to look at him," I snapped back. Warm, wet liquid trickled down my neck, and I reached behind me to find my head was bleeding. *Great.* "Did you really have to hit me?"

"Go to sleep and stay away from him." He clapped a lower hand on my shoulder and shoved me away from the cage. I stumbled forward, tripping over a root, and just barely caught myself from face planting. I turned to glare at him, but Kutzal caught my attention.

One hand was braced behind his head, fingers digging into his hair, and he stared at me as if he'd never seen me before. With my empty skin clutched in my head, I retreated to my tree trunk to nurse my head wound and try to get some sleep.

But those purple eyes didn't leave me. Even as I lay down on my side, I could still feel him watching me. That night, I dreamed of golden smoke.

THREE

KUTZAL

I didn't sleep that night. I lay on my side facing the sleeping female. Trix. Her eyes moved from beneath her thin eyelids, and her face twitched as if she dreamed. I wondered what she dreamed about, and then wanted to smash my face against the bars for giving a shet.

Now I understood why I'd been so captivated by that stupid flecking arrow when we'd found it in our camp and the females had said it belonged to their friend. This Trix... this fierce archer... was my mate.

I rubbed the back of my head, which still echoed with pain from the blow Trix had received from the Joktal guard. I knew little about the cora-eternal commitment, or mating at all for that matter, but I knew that once an enemy spilled the blood of a female, and I felt the pain as if I'd been struck... that was the beginning of the bond. The last step was to kill the one who spilled her blood. The Joktal who hit her lay flat on his back, arms flung out at the sides, his maw opened as he snored.

I couldn't kill him. Whatever happened, I could *not* complete this bond. A mate was the last thing I wanted. My entire clavas of warriors could find their mates and that would be fine, but me? *No*, no way would I, could I bond myself to a female. This planet was too harsh and our civilization too fragile. I could barely keep my warriors and myself safe. I couldn't bear losing and burying another female who meant so much to me.

I closed my eyes as I fought against the dizzying wave of nausea. Why was this happening? And of all females, it was *this* one who clearly had a death wish and who trusted the wrong flecking species. Not that I could blame her. She thought she was helping her friends, and one thing I'd learned about these females was that they were fiercely loyal to each other.

So why had she touched me? Given me water? I also couldn't understand why she'd reacted so badly to my grip on her wrist. I hadn't squeezed that hard, and while she'd held in a cry, her eyes had teared in agony.

I rolled on my back and folded my hands behind my head. I had to get out of this cage. And as much as I didn't want to spend more time than necessary, I'd have to take her with me. *She is All* was the Drixonian creed, and no matter what, those were the words I lived by. While I wasn't sure I liked human females, I still revered them.

Although this one... she wasn't like Amber and Tasha. She didn't smile as freely, and her language was cruder. When she'd brushed the back of my hand with careful fingers, I'd felt the touch spread out to every limb like wildfire.

I didn't understand what that was. As a son of naught, I

hadn't received the standard warrior mating lessons on how to pleasure females as we weren't meant to procreate. So, my reaction to her touch was unfamiliar and uncomfortable. But yet... I wanted it again.

"Fleck," I muttered, rubbing my hands over my face. I had to get my head straight. I couldn't be worrying about the female's feelings toward me or my feelings toward her. Feelings were useless.

There wasn't time to convince the female to trust me, and even if we could communicate, I wasn't sure I had the patience to do so. I could only control myself, which meant it was up to me to get free. That was all that mattered. Pay attention. Plan. Escape. I wasn't voted drexel of the outcasts for nothing.

It was another day before I had my chance. While I didn't scout the borders as much as some of my warriors, I knew the area well. I'd lived here a long time ago, and this land was familiar. We ran parallel to the border with the common lands, so we remained in Wutark and Joktal territory on purpose—once we crossed the borders, one of my warriors would see and sound the alarm. Confident they could hold me, Upreth had been free with his words to his guards. So, I knew he wanted to surprise my clavas at our camp.

At dusk the next evening, about half of the guards, along with Upreth, left to hunt game as the food stores were dwindling. The guard who'd struck Trix was part of the hunting party, making this the perfect time to free myself without having to kill him and bond myself to the female.

And the best part? The hunting party had taken the hounds.

The remaining guards began to make camp—starting a fire and setting out bed rolls. The female sat by herself with her legs crossed, gaze flitting between me and the guards, as she ate a bowl of cold stew.

Earlier that day, I'd found a meal bar in my cage, and later half a skin of water. I knew it was the human leaving me food. It seemed the Joktals had no intention of feeding me on any sort of regular schedule.

"Shouldn't you feed him?" The female called out suddenly.

I went still. I didn't care about food, but I needed one of the guards to come near my cage. Sticking a hand inside would be even better.

"Why?" One grunted.

"What's the point in capturing him if he dies before we get to his camp?" she asked. "I didn't risk my life to shoot him for no reason."

The guard who usually positioned himself at my cage stood, and the keys on his belt rattled. My cora sped up as he dished a splash of stew in a bowl and began to walk toward my cage.

He angled it to fit through the bars of the cage and dropped it so that the bowl upended. The meager amount of stew splattered on my boots.

"There," the guard sneered. "Are you hungry? Lick it up, mongrel."

I stared at him impassively but coiled my muscles to prepare for action. When I didn't respond to his taunts, he reached through the bars of my cage and shoved the bowl closer to me. "Come on—"

He didn't get one more word out. I grabbed his arm and

yanked. His body hit the bars outside the cage. My unleashed machetes slipped through the bars and slammed into the soft skin under his chin. Joktal blood spurted around my blades. His eyes bulged as he struggled weakly.

"Danith?" One guard called from nearby the fire. "Are you okay?"

I tugged my machets free of his chin and right before he dropped, I snatched the keys off his belt. As soon as he hit the ground with a gurgled thud, the remaining Joktal guards raced toward my cage.

But they were too slow. I had the key in the lock and turned before they made it halfway. Leaping out of the cage, I hit the dirt in a crouch and surged up just as the first guard made it to me. I slashed my machets across his neck and he arched away with a cry.

A whip wrapped around my leg, and I smelled the sizzle of burnt cloth a moment before the pain of the charged weapon sliced into my thigh. With a grunt, I sliced through the whip with my machets, and the end turned brown before it fell away.

Two guards approached me at once, and I felt a blade tear into my injured shoulder just as a bony plate slammed into my back. I lashed out with my tail, catching the Joktal behind me and tugging him off his feet. I punched the Joktal in front of me and immediately regretted that decision. His head was like a solid wall, and I definitely did more damage to my fist than I did to his face.

He sneered at me, and I ducked just before taking a bony plate to the face. Snatching a knife off his belt, I slammed it into his thigh. He hollered and staggered back. Whirling around, I slammed my machets down into the face of the Joktal behind me. Again and again, I stabbed him with my sharp blades until his face was a mess of blood and flesh.

Facing the last Joktal, I pulled the blade from his thigh and then slammed it into his neck. He staggered, spit up blood, and then crumpled to the ground.

My shoulder ached, my thigh was on fire, and I was seeing double. I had to get the fleck out of here before the hunting party returned. Turning around, I halted abruptly as I faced an arrow aimed directly between my eyes.

Bow strung taut, feet planted, the human female stared at me with a clenched jaw. Her arm quivered slightly as she faced off against me, and a fierce bolt of respect surged through me. She'd seen me slice through five Joktal guards, but she didn't back down from threatening me.

She swallowed thickly before shifting her stance slightly. But her bow didn't waver, and that arrow would pierce my skull if she let it fly. She kicked something toward me, and I glanced down to find my implant updater.

"Choose your language and toss it back to me," she ordered.

Keeping my gaze on her, I bent down and grabbed the updater. After spinning the dial to my language, I rolled the updater back to her.

She seemed unsure of her next step. In order to update her implant, she'd have to lower her bow. But lowering her bow meant opening herself up to what she considered a threat—*me*.

As much as we didn't have time for this, I realized the female wasn't content to be a pawn in this game between the Joktals and me. I needed her trust, and she seemed desperate to want someone she could trust.

So, I held my hands out, palms up, and stepped away from her. Then I turned my back to her. She could decide to send that arrow into my back or my head, but I had to believe that the female who left me food and water would hear me out before ending my life. I closed my eyes. And I waited.

Trix

This ranked up there as one of the scariest moments of my life, and that was saying something based on all the shit I'd been through.

I'd just seen this Drixonian leap from his cage with deadly black blades emerging from his forearms, head, and down his back. He'd taken down five guards on his own, even while stabbed, punched, and whipped. The mark on his thigh oozed and bubbled, and I couldn't imagine how badly that hurt, but he walked with barely a limp. His shoulder with the arrow wound was once again bleeding profusely from a knife wound, and blood trickled from his ear. He'd taken some vicious blows to the head.

I knew I needed to act fast, because the hunting party would be back soon, but I couldn't seem to lower my weapon. When I saw the Drixonian get loose, the first thing I'd done was retrieve my weapon from the now unguarded pack, which also held the Drixonian's things. That was where I'd found the implant updater. The fact he'd traveled with one intrigued me.

And then there was the fact that he'd chosen to trust me. He'd turned his back on me, so I felt safer updating my implant.

With my bow still notched, I bent my knees. When the

updater was within reach, I dropped my bow, grabbed it, and jammed it against the implant over my left ear. I steeled myself against the jolt of hot pain, which rendered me immobile for a few minutes. When my eyes focused, I saw Kutzal had turned around. Scrambling to my feet, I notched my bow again, but he remained motionless.

His palms remained in the air as he spoke in a calm, clear voice. "Amber is kind and likes to help with odd jobs around our camp." My heart skipped a beat. "Tasha doesn't like me a whole lot, but she tolerates me. We would never hurt them as that goes directly against what Drixonians stand for."

I blinked back tears. "How do I know you're telling the truth?"

"They talk about you, Lu, Maisie, and Neve. We haven't found them yet after you all were taken by the Wutarks, but we will. We promised Amber and Tasha."

Did I dare believe him? "Upreth showed me a photo of Amber being carried on the back of a Drixonian."

He chewed his lips thoughtfully. "That must have been when she escaped Joktalis with Vinz."

My arms ached from holding the bow taut. The arrow point wavered. "Escaped?"

"She was held at Joktalis and met Vinz who was a prisoner there. They escaped together, and now she's safely at our camp."

I lowered my bow, and he remained where he stood. "You'll take me to them?"

"I won't ask you to act as bait. I won't hurt you. I will take you to your friends."

"I'm keeping my bow and this knife." I held up a blade I'd stolen from the guards' supplies. "And I'll use it if you touch me."

He didn't look impressed or amused. "You saw my machets. A small blade won't harm me."

"Are you trying to convince me to go with you or not?"

A muscle in his jaw jumped. "I have no desire to touch you." Suddenly his head turned, and he cocked it as if listening to something. When he faced me again, his voice held a tinge of urgency that hadn't been there before. "But we need to go. I can hear the hunting party returning."

He rushed past me and grabbed his harness, fur shawl, tail armor, and single weapon—the massive sword that made my tiny blade look puny. In the cage, he had still looked terrifying, but outfitted in his armor and weapons, he was once again that fearsome alien I'd first seen that had struck terror into my bones.

He stared at me with thinly veiled annoyance. "We need to go."

I took a step toward him, nerves racing over my skin like ants. "If you betray me, I'll kill you."

He snorted. "I would expect nothing less." He beckoned with his arm. "Now run, female. Run faster than you ever have, or I'll carry you."

I shuddered at the painful memory of the Wutark's hands on me. No way. No one was carrying me again until I was dead. "Just keep up, Drix," I gritted out.

Bow strapped to my back, blade shoved into my belt, I took off at a dead sprint toward Kutzal. He registered surprise for a moment before he took off into the dense brush. I followed, focusing only on his back as the setting sun glinted on his sword. We wove between trees, sped through streams, and trudged through mudlands. My heart soared as the distance between us and the Joktals widened. There was something about them that had never made me feel right, but I was blinded by the promise of seeing my friends safe and sound. Now, according to Kutzal, the Joktals had promised something they couldn't give me. Only two of my friends were ensconced in the Drix camp. So where were Lu, Maisie, and Neve?

I was just beginning to think we were free and clear when the howl of the Joktal hounds split the darkening sky. By now, the sun was merely a sliver on the horizon, and the eerie howl in the near darkness felt like an arrow in my back. I stumbled and the Drix reached back to help me up but pulled his arm back at the last moment. "Are you okay?" he asked. The fucker wasn't even breathing hard, whereas I felt like I'd run a marathon.

I couldn't hide my heaving breaths as I bent and braced my hands on my knees. I grimaced as the cramp in my side stabbed my guts like a hot poker.

"Fine," I gasped.

"Almost there," he said.

That got me to stand upright. "Where? The camp?"

He shook his head. "We're a couple rotations away. The Joktals will expect us to head straight there." A shadow crossed over his face and his eyes darkened for a moment. "I know a place we can hide. Along the way, we'll disguise our scents."

"How?"

He didn't bother to answer as he turned and took off on a run. With a groan, I followed, hoping like hell I didn't step on something and turn my ankle.

As we ran, the dense brush gave way to a field full of plants that reminded me of closed, green pumpkin flowers, if said flowers were the size of a small sedan. The stems were thicker than my body, and arched about eight feet in the air, but the weight of the flowers bent the plant like a hook so the edges of the massive green petals nearly kissed the ground.

While the girls and I had explored a good bit of the land mass we currently resided on, I'd never seen a plant like this. They smelled of a musty floral perfume, like something I'd have expected my grandmother to wear.

Kutzal stopped in the middle of the field and lifted the edge of a petal. Pointing inside, he said, "Get in."

I blinked at him. "I'm sorry?"

"Get in," he said again.

"Yeah, I heard you. But how—?"

He ignored my question and ducked beneath the petal. The flower shimmied, and one of the petals bulged outward as he struck it with an elbow or his head. "Follow me," he called from inside, his voice muffled.

"This is fucking weird," I muttered before lifting the petal.

Inside, Kutzal sat in a pile of what I could only describe as goo. Cloying, nose-tingling, sense overloading, *goo*. I pinched the bridge of my nose as I fought the urge to gag.

Climbing up inside the flower, I rested my back on the bulbous base while Kutzal closed the bottom of the flower, sealing it with goo so it didn't open and dump us out.

The petals were a thick opaque green, although some moonlight filtered through, and dangling above us like a chandelier was the stamen. Kutzal reached up and snagged an orange stamen tip that crumbled in his hand like a smashed peanut. He placed a few bits in his palm and held it out to me as he tossed the rest in his mouth.

I shook my head. "No thanks." My voice came out nasally as I still had my nose plugged.

His lips twitched, and he let out a little snort. "The juggis secretion will mask our scent."

"I'm pretty sure I'll smell like this for the rest of my life."

"It washes off."

"If you say so." I should have been grateful, but I was merely trying not to pass out. The scent was so strong that even when I inhaled through my mouth, I swore I could taste it. My stomach protested.

I was about to punch my way through the petals to get away from the scent when a nose hound brayed nearby.

My eyes shot to Kutzal's. He stared back at me with his fingers pressed over his lips. Right, I had to be quiet. As much as I wanted to fight, this was the better strategy. We didn't have the element of surprise anymore. We would have to fight half a dozen Joktals plus their nose hounds. Kutzal's wounds still appeared red and angry, although he didn't appear to be favoring them. I gazed across our flower hideout to see his torso was marred with scars. He probably was no stranger to pain, and for some reason that hurt my heart.

He stared back at me, and his Adam's apple bobbed as he swallowed. His violet eyes burned, and his fists clenched and unclenched on his thick thighs. The whip had burned through his pants, so the fabric of one pant leg now remained crumpled around the base of his boot to reveal his scaled thigh and calf. The wound oozed a clear pus, and I worried it was infected.

I scooted closer to him, careful not to jostle the flower and reveal our position. His eyes narrowed at my movements, but he remained still as I slid in the goo next to him. I tore the fabric of his torn pant leg and removed it from the base of his boot. With my teeth, I ripped it into strips. Some, I stowed in my pockets, but I took a few and began to wrap his thigh. I was careful not to touch his skin, but I could feel the heat of his body as I sat close to him.

He sat tense with his arms braced behind him, curled into fists. His breath ruffled the hair on top of my head. I didn't think anything of it until I noticed the groin of his pants begin to tighten as a bulge appeared beneath the fabric.

Tying off the wrap, I yanked my hands back to find he wasn't looking at me. His face was turned away, eyes closed, and his lips moved silently. My skin flushed, and for one absolutely crazy moment that I chalked up to my delirium in this flower, I thought about touching him. Would that bulge be hot in my hand? Would he flash those violet eyes at me with lust?

I swallowed around my suddenly dry throat. "Kutz—"

He cut me off in a raspy voice, "Please move away, female."

FOUR

Kutzal

I needed her to get away from me. She hadn't even touched my skin but the feel of her hands so focused on my thigh messed with my head. And my cock... the flecking thing had never been of use to me. I expelled my liquid waste with it and that was it. I never had the desire to mate and never felt this heated flush to my skin and the thickening bulge in my groin. My balls felt full, and my head spun with the need to release my seed.

I didn't want to touch it, unsure what would happen if I closed my fist around the hard length.

Worst of all, the female saw it. For a moment, she remained motionless, hand poised in the air, before she gave a little nod and returned to her side of the bloom. But it wasn't far enough away. I needed her... on another planet. Despite the overwhelming scent of this plant, I could still smell her—the freshness of her skin and the earthy tones of her hair.

When the footsteps outside came closer, followed by the gruff tones of the Joktals, I lifted my gaze to hers. Our eyes met. Held. Despite the proximity of our enemies and the imminent danger we were in if they found us, the anxiousness zinging under my skin bled away as I stared into her green eyes.

Back at camp, Amber and Tasha spoke easily with the other warriors, and even Tasha had granted us a certain level of trust when she'd first arrived. But Trix wore her distrust and mental guard like physical armor. I didn't think that was because of the lies she'd been told about us. I was sure even if I met her under better circumstances, she would have held me and others at arms' length. In a way, she reminded me of myself.

As she held my gaze, a bit of her wariness faded. The lines around her eyes softened, and her lips—which she usually held pursed and tense—had softened. I shouldn't have cared about that. It didn't matter she remained cautious of me as long as she didn't do anything to jeopardize our escape. But I found that I liked this soft look on her.

"Hounds lost the scent, commander," A Joktal spoke. I recognized his voice as the one who struck Trix and I wished I could plunge my hand through the petal and rip his throat out.

"*How?*" Upreth roared. "They didn't have much of a head start. This can't stand. We must find them. That Drix killed five of my warriors."

I couldn't see their forms in the dark and through the thick petals, but I could tell they spoke nearby. We were right under their noses, and they had no idea. I smirked to myself. Before I killed Upreth, I'd let him know how close he came to catching us, and how I outsmarted him. He didn't know this planet or the vegetation like I did.

The hounds snuffled as Upreth continued to rage. The footsteps retreated, but I didn't move or speak for a long time. Trix's head bobbed as she fought the urge to nod off. She shifted slightly and smacked herself lightly on the cheek before shaking her head.

Taking pity on her, I whispered, "I'll get out first and check to make sure we're clear."

Eyes gleaming, she nodded.

I lifted a petal and hopped to the ground. My clothes and skin were slick with the plant's sticky seed. I slicked off as much as I could before scouting the edge of the field. There were no Joktals in sight, and they hadn't covered their clear tracks that led away from our hiding place.

Jogging back to the plant, I lifted a petal and gestured for Trix to emerge. She tried to exit gracefully but ended up sliding down the petal and landing hard on her hip. "Dammit," she muttered and rose to shake her arms and legs. "What is this stuff? It smells like a floral couch where someone died."

I wasn't sure what those words meant. "The plant's seed."

She froze. "I'm sorry?"

"They secrete this to fertilize—"

"Are you telling me I'm covered in plant jizz?"

"Jizz?"

She waved a hand as she held a hand on her chest and gagged. "Oh gross."

I didn't understand. "What's gross about fertilization? This plant just saved your life."

She straightened and stared at me. I stared back. Finally, she sighed. "You're right." Turning, she patted the large bloom. "I apologize for calling you gross. This is a natural part of life, and I hope you have a fantastic marriage and little plant babies." She stepped closer and lowered her voice, as if worried the plant would overhear. "But in all honesty, can we wash this off? It's giving me a headache."

I didn't prefer the smell either. "Yes, there's a stream nearby."

"Great," she grinned, and the sight caught me off guard. Even with her hair matted to her head and her clothes drenched in the plant seed, her smile shone brighter than the stars.

I stared at her mouth too long, apparently, because she dropped the smile as quickly as she'd flashed it. Clearing her throat, she narrowed her eyes and crossed her arms over her chest. "So? About that bath?"

"Follow me," I snapped, irritated I'd been caught looking.

The stream wasn't far off, and the water sparkled under the moonlight. When we drew close, Trix let out a little exclamation of glee and rushed ahead. She splashed into the qua and then spun on her heels, flung her arms out to the sides, and let out a quiet laugh before falling backward.

She disappeared under the qua, and I ran after her, worried she would wash downstream, when she flapped to the surface and sprayed an arc of qua out of her mouth.

"It's cold as shit, but I would jump in the Arctic right now if it meant washing this off." My face must have betrayed my worry, as she went still and cocked her head. "Were you worried I was going to drown?"

I crossed my arms over my chest as I stood in knee-deep qua. "You were under the surface. I wasn't sure you'd come back up."

"I can swim." Her lips curled in amusement

"Good for you," I snapped. "Don't disappear again." I began to splash qua over my body, face, and hair in order to wash off the sticky seed.

"Bossy," she muttered.

"Do you know what Amber and Tasha would do to me if I returned you harmed in any way? Do you want to know what their mates would do to me if I upset them?"

She stood up so quickly that I thought she saw a Joktal. I whirled around to search the banks. "What? Did you hear something?"

"Yeah, I heard something," she barked. "Mates? Did you say mates?"

I turned back around slowly. Never in my life had I gotten in trouble for giving away too much information. And now I was barely in this female's presence for half a rotation, and I'd already said something I hadn't intended to tell her. Her friends could tell her their life situations; that wasn't my responsibility. So, I went for casual denial and continued to wash myself. "Is that what I said?"

She stomped toward me, and I was impressed such a small creature could make that much noise and displace that much qua. Her bow was in her hand, an arrow notched. When had she done that? "That's exactly what you said, fucker. Explain."

I resisted drawing my machets. That was an act of aggression, and I wouldn't react that way to her, despite her own violent tendencies. She was such a fierce, angry little thing.

When I didn't speak right away, her jaw worked, and I realized that she was less angry and more actively terrified for her friends.

I sighed. "I can explain. But I'd like to do so without an arrow in my face."

"Is there a sign here that declares this stream as your property where you make the rules?"

I'd had enough of her sharp tongue. I reached out and grabbed the bow before yanking it toward me. She lurched forward with a cry and caught herself before smacking into me. Our faces were so close I could feel her breath, and my chest almost brushed hers when I inhaled. The bow remained pressed to my shoulder. "Look female," I growled. "I'm getting tired of you threatening me. We'll have a conversation like flecking adults, or we won't have one at all and I'll carry you back to camp hog-tied and gagged. Is that what you want?"

Her nostrils flared. She struggled to tug the bow from my grip but got nowhere. Grunting in frustration, she peeled back her lips to reveal her blunt teeth in a snarl about as ferocious as a baby salibri. "You're an asshole."

"I think Tasha called me that too. If it's an insult, it's accurate. I don't need you to like me, Trix. I just need you to not want to kill me."

She didn't answer, only huffed out a furious breath.

I cocked my head. "Do you want to kill me?"

"No," she said quickly, and I believed her. She licked her lips. "But I would like to hit you once or twice. A good slap."

I shrugged. "Then slap me."

Her head jerked. "What?"

"Then slap me."

Her brows dipped, and she blinked a few times as her mouth went slack. "Wait, I—uh, I don't really..." Nose scrunched, she stomped her foot. "It's no fun when you know it's coming."

I barked out a laugh and shoved her away. She stumbled back a few steps but lowered her bow. Her bravado had faded, and instead she stood panting slightly while nibbling her lips. When she spoke again, her voice shook. "I just want to know if my friends are safe."

"Very safe," I answered. "They are happy and well cared for. And yes, they have mates. Finish up, and I'll explain. But point that bow at me and it's the gag for you, got it?"

Her shoulders sagged and she curled her lip with a little pout. "Fine. Got it. *Jerk.*"

"I heard that one too," I called over my shoulder. With her facing my back, she didn't see me smile.

Trix

The smell of roasting meat pulled me from my dream where I was kicking the shit out of a punching bag. I opened my eyes to find Kutzal sitting nearby in front of a fire while the sun shone through the blue leaves overhead. Wait, it was morning already?

I sat up quickly to rub my eyes. "What happened?"

He gestured to a pile of cooked meat in front of me on a leaf beside a few berries. "Eat."

As much as I resented his one-word order instead of a proper answer to my question, my stomach rumbled. The food the Joktal had provided me had been nowhere near enough to satisfy me. I was pretty sure they thought my stomach was the size of a pea.

I grabbed a hunk of meat and chewed. I was the hunter

for my friends, so I guessed this was a bilket, which was a small squirrel-like animal that wasn't hard to kill. "Did you... leave me alone while I was sleeping to hunt?"

His eyes shifted to me in annoyance. "Yes, I also let the Joktal know where you are."

I curled a lip at him. "I don't need sarcasm."

"It was a stupid question. Of course, I wouldn't leave you alone. I shot this bilket from where I sat. They are easy prey."

"They are." I bit into a berry.

He pointed to where my bow rested nearby. "I'm assuming you hunt?"

"I was the hunter for the girls, yes. I'm pretty good at it."

"I believe you."

After taking a long sip of water, I got back to my original question. "I don't remember much after we left the stream. What happened?" I touched my head to find I'd never re-braided my hair after washing it. The length was a mass of waves and snarls. I tried to finger comb it and eventually gave up, plaiting it into two braids on either side of my head.

"You were nearly asleep on your feet. I made camp, began to talk as you requested, and you immediately started snoring." It was like he couldn't resist getting a dig in at me when he leaned forward with an added, "Loudly."

This fucker. "Are you making fun of my snoring? What are you, *five*?" I glared with a huff. "Anyway, whatever. I hope my snores were so loud that you couldn't sleep."

He ducked his head, and I expected him to fling another barb at me but instead he muffled a noise behind his hand. His shoulders shook, and I paused mid-braid to bend my neck and peer at his face. "Are you... laughing?"

He lifted his head quickly, face carefully composed. "Of course not."

"I mean... it sounded like a laugh."

His eyes narrowed. "I made no sound."

He was infuriating. "Okay fine, you didn't laugh. You never laugh. Your life is devoid of humor and joy, only battle and pain." I waved a hand and his eyes narrowed to barely slits as if he aimed to take off my head. "So, let's get back to it. Explain to me how my girls are now somehow alien mates. I truly can't *wait* to hear this tale."

A muscle in his jaw ticked. "I don't like your tone."

"Well, my tone doesn't get much better when it comes to the safety of my girls."

"And I don't handle disrespect to my warriors. They're honest males who've been through more than you can imagine."

"And we haven't?" I nearly shrieked. "In case you weren't aware, this isn't my fucking planet. It's not even my *fucking galaxy.*"

He puffed out a breath through his flared nostrils like a bull and I huffed back, at a standstill over our different loyalties. But I had to admit part of my feelings toward Kutzal had shifted. Sure, he was an asshole, but he was loyal. He cared about his warriors and took personal offense to the idea that I thought they'd hurt my friends.

This yelling at each other was stupid and getting us nowhere. I rolled my shoulders to ease the tension out of them and continued to eat. "I will adjust my tone if you respect that my ability to trust has been shattered over and over again since being abducted from Earth."

He exhaled slowly and rubbed at the pierced lobe of his ear. "I respect that you have no reason to trust me. I would say that I don't care, but that's not true. I would like you to trust me."

His eyes shone, and I swallowed as he held my gaze. With a nod, I said, "I will try."

After taking a long sip of his water, he clasped his hands in front of him with his elbows braced on his knees. "First I need to explain a little about us."

"Okay."

He proceeded to give me a bit of background about his race—how they lived on this planet more than a hundred and fifty cycles ago in a matriarchal society. The women comprised the governing body while the men all joined the military to defend their home.

"Our creed is *She is All*," he said, meeting my eyes. "You need to understand that protecting and respecting females is the cornerstone of who we are. So, when a virus swept through our society and killed all our females and most of our elder males, we were distraught. Unorganized. Leaderless. We only knew how to defend, not run adrift. Without the promise of mates and chits, the remaining warriors were hard to corral." He looked down at his hands. "A lot happened after that and I can explain another time, but we had to leave our planet for many, many cycles. Now that we have returned, it's the same but also not. The Wutarks and Joktals claimed part of it for themselves but are not inclined to share. The Wutarks stole you from your camp. They took Tasha to their settlement and planned to use her as a sacrifice."

"A sacrifice?"

He nodded and seemed to choose his words carefully. "The sacrifice would require her death."

I chewed the inside of my cheek as I fought back a howl of rage.

He continued. "Even though he'd been instructed not to enter the Wutark borders, Lukent spied on them and saw

Tasha. He saved her and brought her back to our camp. I could tell Lukent was taken with her, and she was very dependent on him. He'd earned her trust. When I sent her to our city of Granit, where the most powerful clavas is rebuilding, I sent her with another warrior. Along the way she ran from Axton and found Lukent. She refused to leave his side. I expected him to return to our camp alone, but when he arrived, Tasha was at his side. And they were mated."

"...mated? What does that mean?"

He rubbed his wrists in an odd gesture. "Some Drixonians are lucky enough to find their cora-eternals, blessed by Fatas."

"What's Fatas?"

"Fatas is in everyone and everything. We believe she rewards good deeds and punishes bad ones."

I nodded. "Okay, go on."

"Cora-eternals are marked with matching loks, which are golden wrist bands."

"Who gives them these wrist bands?"

He cocked his head at me. "No one, they appear on their skin when the bond is confirmed."

I felt my eyebrows raise. "They just appear?"

He blinked at me as if I was the crazy one. "Yes."

"Does anything prompt this?"

He nibbled his lip, so a white fang poked out. He heaved a breath before answering. "When an enemy spills a female's blood, the male will often feel the pain of the blow. That is the beginning of the bond. When the male kills that enemy... that's when the bond is confirmed and the loks appear. A cora-eternal mating can also feel each other's emotions."

The human part of me that lived on Earth would have

scoffed at all of this. But then I wasn't that human anymore. I'd seen things I'd thought were impossible. The condition of my body was proof enough. "Lukent and Tasha...?"

"Are cora-eternals. So are Vinz and Amber. Vinz was imprisoned by the Joktals where Amber was kept as a servant. Amber helped him escape, and he brought her with him to our camp. They have formed a very close bond, and Amber is a favorite among the other warriors for tempering Vinz."

My eyes pricked with tears, because even those few words about Amber made sense. Of course she was a favorite. She had a huge heart and could make anyone love her.

A sob bubbled up my throat and I placed the back of my hand over my mouth. "Sorry," I mumbled as a few tears spilled out.

He leaned back on his hands. "It's okay. I know humans cry."

"D-do Amber and Tasha cry a lot?" I asked.

His eyes crinkled. "They do when they speak of you and the other females."

Another sob jerked my body, and I ducked my head as the tears rolled down my cheeks. We'd been through so much and to be separated like this broke my heart. "You'll take me to them?"

"Of course."

"Do you know what happened to us?" I sniffed.

His jaw shifted. "I know you were held by the Uldani for many cycles. You should know that the Uldani were responsible for the virus, which they unleashed in order to gain us warriors as their military. We didn't know that at the time, so we agreed to work for them on Torin. It wasn't for many cycles that we realized the Uldani were not to be trusted. We fought them in an Uprising and later defeated their entire city and killed all their elite responsible for the corruption. So, I can tell you that any Uldani who treated you terribly are dead. I know that won't make up for what they did, but I hope it eases some of your anger."

I swallowed. "Did you know about their underground labs?"

His eyes hardened. "We did. Those have been destroyed."

A harsh breath escaped my lungs. "Good."

But he was like a dog with a bone. "What do you know about the labs?"

"I saw them and heard about them. They conducted experiments there on other species."

He didn't need to know that was where I'd lived several years of my life. Amber and Tasha must not have told him about their alters, which would make sense. We'd all agreed they were our own business. And to be honest, I still wasn't sure about the extent of my alter. Skin to skin contact was painful for me, like a hot burn. But sometimes, on rare occasions if I initiated the contact, the pain would be delayed. It varied—sometimes the pain would flare in thirty seconds, sometimes longer. I could never be sure, and I hadn't experimented much because, well, it fucking hurt.

I wasn't sure he believed me, but he dropped the line of questioning. Eager to change the subject, I went back to a question I was curious about. "And is that the desire for all of you? To meet your mates and produce little human/Drix hybrids?"

"I cannot speak for all warriors, but I would say that's a desire for a good amount of them."

I wasn't sure why I wanted to know this, but I kept going. "And you?"

"No." His answer was quick, rapt, and definite. "I do not desire a mate. Ever."

He gave me a look when he said it, as if I alone was responsible for this decision. "I know you don't care for me, but most human women are more likable than me." Not that I wanted any of my friends to have to deal with his grumpy ass all the time.

His eyes settled on me, studying me. "This has nothing to do with whether I like you or not. You have some desirable traits that many warriors—other than me—would find value in as they considered you for a mate."

I was ready to spit fire. Like I gave a shit about being desirable to a Drixonian warrior. *Consider me as a mate?* Fuck that. Long ago, I'd wanted to meet the love of my life and start a family, but then I'd been stolen from Earth and brought here where my body was no longer the same.

"Well, that's nice you deem me as possessing desirable traits, but I'll pass on this mate nonsense. Those loks sound more like shackles of ownership. And *no one* will own me again." The words came out stronger than I intended, and I ducked my head in shame as my voice cracked with conviction.

"Let me rephrase," he said softly. "Any warrior would be lucky to have you as a mate. You are strong, have archery skills, and are intelligent. You also look very appealing. If you desired a mate, you'd have your pick."

My arms broke out in goosebumps, and an ache cramped my stomach. The air grew denser, and I fought to inhale deeply. The thing is... he didn't know me as well as he thought he did. He certainly didn't know that, thanks to the Uldani, I possessed a very undesirable trait that would make having a mate nearly impossible.

"You don't know everything about me." My voice didn't sound like my own.

His tongue probed the corner of his mouth before he answered, "I know all I need to know. And Trix, I promise, as long as I live, you'll never be owned again."

His eyes held mine, and the ache in my stomach bled away into a familiar and surprising heat. My heart pounded loudly in my ears as a bead of sweat dripped down the back of my neck. Had the temperature increased in the last minute or so? Why was I so affected by his words?

Suddenly, his nose scrunched like he'd tasted something bad. "No more of this. Being nice to you makes my head hurt."

And just like that, the tension broke. My lungs inflated with fresh air as I let out a relieved bark of laughter. "Yeah, your compliments make me want to hurl."

He shivered, but his eyes held just a hint of amusement. "Good, we're in agreement."

"Yes, never do that again."

"Never. You're an annoying female who shot me."

"And you're a giant asshole who threatened to gag me."

"That threat remains in effect." His lips twitched.

"And I still have my bow and arrows." I patted them beside me. "So, watch your tongue, Drix."

Eyes glittering, he leaned froward. "And you watch yours, female."

FIVE

Trix

I was determined to get this mondril before Kutzal. Because we were both too alpha to wait at camp, we'd decided that we'd *both* hunt for our next meal. Whoever got the game first won. Won what? Bragging rights. And in my weird relationship with Kutzal, bragging rights meant everything. I didn't know why I felt like I had to prove myself to him, but I did.

The mondril had a densely muscled body about the size of a hog. Snorting up a storm, the green-furred animal ran on two bird-like legs. I'd never chased an ostrich, but I imagined it was sort of like this, if an ostrich was a mammal with a snout and pointy ears.

It ducked and weaved among the trees. I crashed through the foliage, not bothering to keep quiet. The mondril knew I was on its tail. It was just a matter of time before one of us tired. I hoped it wasn't me.

I let an arrow fly when I thought I had a shot, but the

arrow flew wide and stuck into the trunk of a tree with a solid thunk. Cursing under my breath, I snatched it out as I ran by. I couldn't waste arrows.

A rustle to my right drew my attention long enough to see Kutzal to my left racing toward the same prey.

"Hey, find your own fucker!" I shouted at him, but he only shot me a feral grin before running harder.

"Goddamnit," I huffed. He was faster than me, but I wasn't going out without a fight.

Suddenly the mondril banked a hard right, sending us in a totally different direction, and I took off after it.

"Trix!" He bellowed after me.

I whooped with glee. He was *so pissed* I was going to win. I could tell the mondril was tiring and as soon as I got an open shot, the little animal was going to be dinner.

I notched my bow and arrow and just as we burst out into a small clearing, I stopped, planted my feet, and took aim at the furry butt. I let the arrow fly, but at the last minute, the mondril turned a hard left and avoided sudden death. The arrow went sailing into a nest of vines. With a hard thwack, it stuck into something solid behind the vines, and the end quivered.

Frowning, I crept forward and yanked out my arrow. Through the vines, I detected planks of wood nailed together in what could only be made by an intelligent species. "What is this?" I whispered to myself as I tugged a section of vines aside to reveal a door.

Stepping back, I studied the vines more closely and realized there was some sort of cabin underneath the plant life—it certainly hadn't been inhabited for many years, but someone at one point had built it with a purpose. I pressed on the door, and it swung inward just as loud footsteps came crashing into the clearing behind me. I turned around to see Kutzal standing just at the edge of the clearing, chest heaving.

"I missed the mondril, but I found something better." I brandished my arm at the door with a grin. "We can sleep here tonight."

With dark eyes and a face devoid of color, he rasped out a quick, "No."

I frowned. "What? Why?"

"We need to leave." He took a step forward and then seemed to flinch as if shocked by an electric fence.

"Why?" I asked again. "Is this the home of something that's going to eat us?"

His chest heaved. "No."

A breeze swung the door open further with a creak. Dust swirled in the beam of sunlight, shining on a spot on the floor. Blue weeds poked up through the floorboards, but a hint of red and purple caught my eye.

I took a step inside and brushed the weeds aside to reveal a large stone with a child-like drawing in vivid colors untouched by the sun. The five figures were unmistakable— blue and black aliens with black horns and long dark hair. The two adults wore dresses, and one held a baby. Of the other two children, one had a bare chest and wore pants while the other wore a dress.

I rose slowly and peered outside at Kutzal who remained where he was standing while staring at the stone as if it was a poisonous snake. My heart pounded. I should have left when he told me too, but I had always been too curious for my own good. Maybe he knew the family who had lived here.

"Kutzal?" I asked gently, taking a step outside.

He didn't react to his name. His body seemed to shake, and his eyes had dulled to a nearly matte black. Shit. What had I done? I took another step toward him. "I'm sorry," I said softly, "I should have listened when you told me to leave."

But it was like I wasn't even there. He seemed to sway on his feet just as his gaze slid with an agonizing slowness to a spot beside the cabin. I followed his sightline to see a large boulder with markings carved in it.

Kutzal bucked forward, and his legs seemed to carry his reluctant body toward the stone, where he fell to his knees as if boneless.

I hurried next to him as he knelt with his head bowed and his hair covering his face.

Crouching next to him, I bit my lips as I studied the stone. There were four separate markings on the boulder, and each etching appeared to be made at a different time, as the scratchings were differently shaped and hadn't weathered with the same consistency. I thought back to the stone. Five figures... four markings... was this a grave? And if so... who was the survivor?

With dread building in my gut, I slowly turned to Kutzal. He stared at the stone with eyes opened to mere slits. He swallowed thickly a few times before reaching out and brushing his fingers over the highest marking. "We lived here away from the rest of the Drix villages, but my grandmother still contracted the virus and died within one rotation. Next was my older sister." His fingers traveled to the next marking. "Then my... baby sister." His hand shook and he fisted it on his thigh as he bent forward with his eyes squeezed shut.

"Last was my mother," he whispered, and opened his eyes long enough to brush his fingers over the last marking.

Tears flowed down my cheeks as empathy bled through me. "How old were you?"

"About four."

My throat closed. I pictured a small Kutzal with nubs for horns and a stubby tail carving his mother's name in this rock. All alone. A child. His hands probably shook then. He must have been out of his mind with grief and so scared.

"I didn't want to leave," he said. "I made traps to catch my food and tried to keep the cabin clean just how my mother liked it. But they still came for me when it was time to leave this planet. I had no choice."

This cabin had been a source of pride for him and his family. Their final resting place was now overrun with weeds.

"You want to know why I don't want a mate?" He turned his head, and I held back a gasp at the naked anguish shone there. "This planet is too volatile, and our survival here is too fragile." He gritted his teeth. "I won't lose another female who has a part of me." He thumped his chest. "I *refuse*."

I nodded, unable to speak without sobbing. I rubbed my damp palms on my pants and reached a tentative hand toward him. He watched my fingers as they brushed the back of his hand, and when no pain flared, I laid my hand on top of his where it rested on his thigh. That touch was all I dared. At first, he didn't move a muscle, but his gaze remained where we connected. And then slowly, he turned his hand until his palm met mine. I laced my fingers between his thick ones. I hadn't held hands with anyone for years. Maybe longer.

I kept expecting the pain to consume my hand and travel up my arm until it stole my breath, but when the pain never came, I finally lifted my gaze to Kutzal's. The lines around his eyes had softened, and when he spoke next, his voice was so quiet, I barely heard it. "Thank you," he murmured.

I shifted closer, and together we bowed our heads in honor of his family.

Kutzal

When Trix withdrew her hand from mine, I immediately missed the warmth. I curled my fingers in my palm as I stared at the rock memorial for my family. The pain of their loss had never really faded, it had just twisted and warped inside my body into something ugly and isolating.

We'd all lost our families, so I wasn't unique, but most had the support of their villages. After being branded a son of naught, my mother refused to see me treated like Lukent was. I remembered being so sad to leave him when we'd packed up and ventured out on our own. My mother and grandmother built the cabin with their bare hands. Alone, we hadn't been aware of the virus until a messenger came to tell us. And that messenger brought said virus to our doorstep.

One by one, they'd died until I was the only one left. Every death had been a blow so strong that once my mother was gone, I'd expected to die next. I hadn't known at the time that the virus killed mostly females. I'd waited to die, alone in the cabin, until I'd been forced to feed myself.

I had vowed then that I'd never lose another female. I wouldn't have a mate or a family. As a son of naught, I'd never expected one anyway.

Scuffling behind me drew my attention and I turned to

find Trix ripping the vines off the walls of the cabin to reveal two windows. She swiped her hands together and then propped them on her hips. "Some light will help, right?"

I didn't answer, unsure what she was doing. But then she marched right inside. What followed was more thumping, a few swear words, and then a bundle of weeds came flying out of the open door.

I forced myself to stand even though my body felt weighed down and made my way to the doorway of the cabin. Inside, Trix was hard at work. She'd found an old broom of my mother's and was busy sweeping out the fire pit in the center of the floor. "It's not so bad." She glanced up at me, and a streak of green dirt marred her forehead. Another marked her chin. "Just needs a little, uh, inside gardening and some sweeping."

I finally found my voice. "You don't have to do this."

She leaned on the handle of the broom and blew a stray strand of hair out of her eyes. "You said your mom liked to keep this cabin clean?"

I nodded. "She built it with my grandmother."

Trix's chin went up and out with a defiant jut. "Then we clean it for her."

Her tone was so matter of fact as she went back to sweeping, and she made a sound in her throat that rose and fell in pitch. In the other corner was a chest, and I didn't dare to think that our belongings remained inside. I'd taken a few things with me to Torin, but not much. Surely someone had raided this cabin long ago. Stopping in front of it, I swiped off the thick layer of dirt, undid the latch, and lifted the lid.

My breath caught. I wasn't sure that I could do this. Not now. Not after retelling the truth of my past to Trix. I'd look through it again before we left. I slowly lowered the lid, once again sealing off the light from my sister's doll. Its eyes seemed to stare back accusingly.

When I rose, Trix's head jerked down, and she resumed sweeping. She cleared her throat. "We don't have to sleep here if you don't want. And you don't have to help me clean. If you want to go hunt for our dinner, I'll take care of this."

"I want to help," I blurted out.

Her eyebrows lifted as she stopped mid-sweep. "You do?"

"I'll work on the walls and roof to tear down the weeds."

She grinned. "Great idea. This isn't a big cabin, and it's only one room. I'll have it cleared out in a jiffy."

I didn't know what a *jiffy* was. "Okay."

She smiled at me, and for some reason, this smile raised the hair on the back of my neck. I paused. "Are you only being nice because you pity me?" My voice came out harsher than I'd intended.

Her smile faded, but she didn't frown. Or yell. "No," she answered casually. "I don't pity you. I think now I understand you. At least a little bit." She chewed the inside of her cheek. "It was brave to share with me what happened to you and your family."

"So, I could kill half a dozen Joktals and that wasn't brave but this was?"

Now she did frown. "There are different kinds of brave. And this..." she gestured outside toward the rock. "I think that was the bravest thing I've seen you do."

She might have understood me, but I wasn't sure I understood her. "Humans are interesting," I mumbled.

Laughing, she went back to sweeping. And I went outside to help clean the cabin.

The smoke from the fire filtered through the hole in the roof as I picked the last bit of meat from the roasting mondril and handed it to Trix.

The cabin was cleaner than I expected was possible. Not likely up to my mother's standards, but after sitting empty for more than a hundred cycles, it looked pretty flecking good.

The water pump still worked, and we'd washed up before sitting on some clean fern bedding to eat the mondril I'd caught. I wished I had a bit of spirits to wash down my dinner, or maybe some of the yuza that Baki grew. I could use something to make my mind fuzzy for just a bit.

The sun had long since fallen, and the stars twinkled through the smoke above us as the fire crackled.

Trix stretched out on her side with her head propped on her fist. She'd stripped down to her pants and a thin fabric band wrapped around her chest. Even her feet were bare. She wiggled her toes as she finished her meat as she once again made that noise in her throat that raised and lowered in pitch. I'd asked her what she was doing earlier, and she'd called it *humming*.

I'd never seen her this relaxed... or happy for that matter. We hadn't talked much this afternoon and instead worked quietly side by side. Amicably. Without arguing. I had relied on her prickliness as my own armor. If she kept me at arm's length, then I could do the same. But now that she was so close that her toes brushed my hip, it was flecking with my head.

"You said you moved away from your village," she asked. "Why's that?"

Of all questions about my past, this wasn't one that

made me angry. I'd long since shed the shame of the sons of naught brand. "In the traditional Drixonian society, all males were drafted to the military of defense. If a warrior deserted, which was considered one of the worst offenses, his family was punished, most specifically his sons. We were labeled the sons of naught and while we were still ordered to serve, we were not given high-level positions. In fact, we were given the worst positions, and the females of the family were stripped of all important titles."

Her toes had stopped wriggling. She certainly wasn't happy and relaxed now. "You're kidding."

"I'm not." I shoved my hair to the side and turned so she could see the back of my neck. "I have the brand to prove it."

"They *branded* you too?" Her voice ended on a shout that made me wince.

"A long time ago. We also were not allowed to have mates or chits. All the members of my clavas are sons of naught. Lukent, Vinz, Axton... all of them."

"So, things have changed, then, right? Because Lukent and Vinz have mates."

"Yes, the head drexel of the remaining clavases is Dazeem Bakut, and while I'd always respected him, I hadn't expected him to be relaxed about the sons of naught. It was important to me as the drexel of the Lone Howl clavas to protect my warriors from further hurt, so I was cautious of Daz. But he has so far treated us well. We still feel like outcasts from the other warriors as we were raised differently than them, but at least this won't carry through to future generations."

"You're the drexel? What does that mean?"

"After we gained independence from the Uldani, the Drix warriors separated into clavases. I was elected the leader, or drexel, of the sons of naught and I promised my warriors I wouldn't let them be treated as disposable again."

"I'm sorry," she said in a quiet tone. "What happened when you were under the thumb of the Uldani? Did they treat you differently?"

My teeth ground together. "Yes."

She sat up with her legs bent to the side. The smooth skin of her stomach stretched over her muscles, distractingly. "How so?"

"We were treated as the disposable warriors. A lot of us were less skilled as we hadn't undergone the training the other warriors had. Some of us..." I swallowed. "Some of us saw the inside of those labs you mentioned."

She leaned even closer, and her breathing quickened. "Did you?"

I met her eyes. "I did not."

She slumped, relieved. "I'm so glad." Her lips moved as she gazed into the fire, and I got the sense she wasn't done talking so I waited her out.

Finally, her stare swung to me. "I guess if you were brave today, then I can be brave too."

I frowned. "What does that mean?"

She let out a shaky breath. "I know about the labs because that was where I was kept. For years."

My fingers curled into fists and my claws dug into my palms as I fought to remain calm. Vinz had been kept there, and while I wasn't entirely sure what had been done to him, I had a few guesses. And none of them were good. "What did they do to you?" My voice rasped out hoarsely.

"They wanted humans to heal faster. When they injured me... on purpose... they thought it took too long for the bruises to fade, the cuts to heal and the bones... to mend." I made a choking sound that twisted Trix's features into a grimace. "So, they tried to change me... make me heal. And all they did was cause me more pain."

I felt like her voice was in a tunnel. All I could picture was Trix in a lab, the sound of her bones breaking, the smell of her blood, her cries of pain. I wanted to scream.

"The reason I told you not to touch me," she bit her lip. "Was because I can't be touched. Skin to skin contact causes me pain."

I stared at her, unable to breathe, remembering how I'd grabbed her wrist when she'd reached through the bars of my cage and how her face had twisted in pain. Disgust and anger over what had been done to her curled my lips. I'd thrown my warrior's pain in her face while all this time, she'd been tortured. And I understood now all the more reason why she refused to be owned, why she wanted full control over herself and her body.

She huffed out a bitter laugh and turned away from me. "I see that look on your face. Still think I'd make a desirable mate to some warrior?"

If I'd been able to grab her chin and jerk her to face me, I would have. Instead, I barked out, "Look at me."

She responded, probably more out of instinct than obedience. Her brows were lowered and she once again wore that mask of ice.

"I don't give a fleck about your desirability as a mate. I'd burn down the entire planet of Torin if I thought I could erase your pain." Her mouth dropped opened, but I wasn't done. "I didn't understand you earlier when you said I was brave, but now I get it. I get it because all I see as look at you is an intelligent, loyal female who is just as valuable as any of my Drixonian warriors. I'll protect you like I protect them—with my life."

SIX

Trix

My heart thrummed in my chest as my attention, my vision, hell my entire *world* tunneled down to this male in front of me. He was still blue with horns and a tail, but he was also, at his core, a soul that I'd miraculously connected with in this strange situation.

I hadn't wanted to like him. I'd have been perfectly fine hating him, but I couldn't deny that our odd relationship had shifted today into... something.

He'd more or less given me the honor of calling me one of his warriors. Not a female he was bound by duty to protect, not a walking womb, but as a person with valuable skills.

And that mattered to me. Maybe it shouldn't have, but it wasn't like I'd arrived in this galaxy with hunting and bow skills. I'd taught myself so my girls and I could survive.

Goosebumps broke out on my arms as our eyes locked. I hadn't realized how close we were, but from here I could feel the damp heat of his breath on my face. The muscles in his neck remained tight and corded, and the intensity with which he focused on me made me feel a bit like prey. And for the first time in my life, I didn't feel scared of the predator in front of me.

Heat swirled in my belly, confusing my senses. The fire seemed to get hotter and hotter, and sweat dripped between my breasts as my nipples pebbled against the thin fabric of my chest wrap. I swallowed, but my mouth had gone dry. Kutzal's gaze broke mine to home in on my throat before sliding down my chest. There, he paused, and a shiver rippled over the skin on his back.

His chest heaved, and his stomach expanded and contracted rapidly over his muscles. It was then I saw the bulge in his pants. I thought I'd seen it before, when we hid in the plant, but this was unmistakable.

Kutzal was hard.

My gaze shot back up to his face to see his eyes had gone dark, and the color on his cheeks had deepened to a muddy purple.

"Leave," he barked out with enough urgency to scare me out of my skin.

"Look—"

"It'll go away if you leave." He didn't seem to know where to look. My face, then my chest, then the fire. His eyes rolled in his head, and he seemed half out of it as he bent over and winced like he was in pain.

I slowly gathered my feet under me. I hadn't listened to him the last time he'd given me an order. It had ended up being a good thing, but this... this didn't seem like something to press Kutzal on.

But I couldn't seem to make myself move. I couldn't

stop looking at the bulge in his pants which seemed to jerk under my gaze.

"*Female!*" He roared, and that got me to my feet. I stumbled a few steps, feeling feverish and achy. My breasts felt full and my inner thighs damp. This wasn't... how could I be reacting so strongly to him?

I took a step toward the door of the cabin when he let out a soft groan. With my hand on the doorframe, I turned back around to see him hunched over with one hand braced on the floor, the other fisted against his groin.

"Just go on," I said quietly. "Get yourself off. It's okay."

His head turned, and his lips were peeled back into a snarl. "What?"

I made a hand-job gesture. "Just do it."

He stared at me like I was crazy. "Do what?"

A tight band wrapped around my chest as I turned fully.

His nostrils flared. "I thought I told you—"

"Do you know how to make yourself come?" I asked him.

Every line in his body was tense. "I haven't been hard like this. Ever."

I tried to hide my shock, but I wasn't sure I succeeded. Crouching down, I pushed his hair out of the way so I could better see his face. "What do you mean?"

"Our females died and so... did our desires."

I felt the blood drain from my face. "Oh my God," I whispered. "Are you... have you ever...?"

"I've never touched a female." He didn't seem embarrassed by that admission. He only seemed angry at his aroused state. Which understandably, was probably a little scary to a full-grown man.

I shook out my hands. I couldn't believe I was about to

suggest this, but he was in pain. As someone who lived in fear of pain, I couldn't just let him suffer. And I didn't know what his anatomy was like. Maybe his balls would burst or something if he didn't climax.

"Sit back against the wall," I instructed.

Grimacing, he studied me for a moment before complying. His eyes still roamed my body, as if he was incapable of not peeking, and that didn't help my situation either. Because underneath the thin layer of pain was undeniable lust. I hadn't realized I was capable of those feelings, but my body had reacted before my brain could keep up. Ridiculously, I wanted to know what his cock felt like in my hand.

He slowly positioned himself slumped against the wall, and now that I was nearby, his eyes fell to half-mast as his heated gaze roamed my body. I'd never felt this desirable in my life, and I wasn't even naked. What would he act like near a bare pussy? He'd probably lose his mind.

"Lower your pants," I murmured.

His nubbed brows dipped for a moment, and his fingers twitched first before finally complying. He winced a few times as he unclasped the belt at the base of his tail and then lowered the waist of his pants to mid-thigh.

His light blue cock sprang free, and the mushroom head dripped copiously with a thin, clear liquid like the best lube money could buy. I could barely believe it. No spit needed.

His balls hung below, full and round with the skin stretched tight over the sacs. He had no hair, and while his cock was more girthy than a human's, it wasn't that uniquely different except for a protruding bump at the upper base of his cock.

I'd touched him earlier and I hadn't felt pain for a long time... the longest stretch I'd ever had.

You can do this, Trix. You can do this.

The thing was, I *wanted* to do it. I ached to touch him so badly that I felt my core clench with need. Right now, he watched me like I held the secret to eternity in my palm as I reached for his cock. It jerked against his stomach, smearing the clear fluid on the ridges of muscle there.

Swallowing my nerves, I let my fingers brush the wet, silky head of his cock. A string of the thin liquid stretched between my finger and his tip. From just that one light touch he moaned, his abs contracted.

"Trix," he whispered in anguished lust. "What... what will you do?"

His tone held a bit of reverence, and I marveled that right here, right now, I was in control. I was the expert. I could show this man, on his home planet and galaxy, something new.

"This." I wrapped my fingers around his shaft and squeezed.

He growled low in his throat and his legs jerked, one booted foot nearly catching me in the thigh. I shifted so I knelt next to him at his hip, away from any uncontrollable limbs.

I felt no pain as I stroked up his hot shaft. His scaly skin had a slight furry texture over a hard casing, like a short velour. When I got to the mushroom tip, I twisted my wrist, and he kicked out again as he choked out a gasp. I'd never ever been with anyone who reacted to a hand-job like this, and I found I *loved* it. I focused on every reaction he had—when he gasped, when he moaned, and when he shuddered as I continued to stroke his cock. When I touched his balls with my other hand, he let out a keening cry and threw his head back.

"Are you..." he gasped out with his eyes squeezed shut and his teeth clenched. "Doing *this* out of pity?"

There was a vulnerability there in his tone, and in the way he avoided my eyes. So, I answered honestly. "Nothing about this is about pity."

His eyes met mine, and I wasn't sure what he saw there, but he let out a shaky breath before rasping, "I want to... please... let me taste you."

"*Taste?*"

He panted like he had just run around the entire planet. "Your cunt, Trix. Let me taste you off your fingers."

My breath left my lungs in a rush, and I felt a rush of wetness dampen my pants. "I—"

"Can you do this to yourself?"

"Can I make myself climax?"

He nodded eagerly, and my hand went still on his cock. "Do you want me to...?"

"Touch yourself. Come. And then let me taste. I can't touch you but... you can touch yourself."

"Oh my God," I breathed, unable to do anything as my stomach cramped. Releasing his cock, I unbuckled my belt and reached my hand into my pants. I was in some sort of fever dream now—that was really the only explanation. I touched my clit and my entire body jerked. My high-pitched cry was more of a whine as I swirled my finger over the engorged bundle of nerves. It wasn't as good as something long and thick filling me, but I was so keyed up and turned on that it didn't take long before the tingle of an orgasm began building in my lower spine.

"That's it," he murmured, his tongue lolling out of his mouth. I fixated on the piercings there, imagining those rolling around my clit. "I can smell your wet cunt from here. You're dripping, aren't you?"

The noise I made wasn't human as my hips jerked, my fingers spasmed, and then I was coming as I rubbed my clit in timing with the pulses of my orgasm. Exhausted, muscles like noodles, I slapped my free hand on the floor. Breathing hard, and just barely sated, I pulled my hand from my pants.

My juices glistened there, and my fingers were nearly prune-like from the moisture.

"Fleck," he rasped out. "Let me taste. Please, Trix."

I lifted my hand to his mouth, and I wasn't even that close to his lips when his long tongue snaked out and wrapped around my fingers. I yelped, expecting pain at the touch, but none came as he tugged them into his mouth. His lips closed around my fingers near my knuckles and then he proceeded to suck and lap at them in the heat of his mouth. He *ate* at them like they were my pussy, and I couldn't believe that my core clenched again at the thought of feeling his tongue there. He moaned and hummed delighted, pleased sounds and I swore a slight rumbling emanated from his chest. Suddenly, his eyes popped open, and the sound stopped. He released my fingers and I drifted them down his chest, over his abs, until once again I reached his groin.

Grasping his cock, I tugged, and when his hand settled over mine, I felt just a licking heat of pain that abated quickly.

Together, we stroked him, and his cock began to swell in our hands. "I can still taste you on my tongue," he panted. "Wish I could spend all day between your thighs drinking that sweetness."

"Kutzal." I could do nothing but say his name, and it came out as a plea. He had to stop. This was already too intense, and my feelings were jumbled with this physical craving and the real need to maintain a distance.

"Trix," he hissed out. I gripped harder. Stroked faster,

and when I swiped my finger over the tip of his cock, he nearly went feral. He kicked out. His hips bucked, and then his cock pulsed like a strobe light. White cum spurted from the tip, landing on his collarbone, his chest, and his abs. The smell of him perfumed the air, and the sweet smell of his release surprised me.

His hands fell limply to his sides, and I released him to slump down onto my hip. My head rested on the wall near his, and I could have slept there, just like that, with the smell of our releases surrounding us.

"Did you have any pain?" he whispered in a soft voice.

And just like that, my heart lurched. After all that, he was worried about me. I shook my head. "None."

He nodded, and his eyes fell to his abs. He dragged a few fingers through his release.

I was too tired to feel awkward. "Are you okay?"

He lifted his head. "Do I look okay?"

"You look better than okay."

He let out a husky laugh. "There's your answer."

I didn't want to talk about happened. Lust had been a driving force there, right? It was just... a physical release that we'd given to each other. I refused to look into this further. At least not tonight.

I crawled toward our fern nest and lay down with my hands tucked under my head. I closed my eyes, and after a moment, I heard rustling and then felt his breath as he settled near me.

I pretended to be asleep, and just when I thought he had fallen asleep too, I felt a finger brush a lock of hair off my forehead. "Thank you," he whispered so softly I barely heard him. "Every day you reveal new skills."

I heard him roll over, and that was when I left myself smile at his back.

SEVEN

Kutzal

I woke to Trix crouched near the fire stirring a pot of something delicious and bubbling. When I moved, the ferns rustled, and she glanced over her shoulder with a cautious smile. "I used the bones of the mondril we had last night and dug up a few root vegetables to make a soup."

"You didn't wander too far from the cabin, did you?"

She shook her head.

"Good," I mumbled as I slid closer to her. "The Joktals are likely still searching for us."

"I know," she answered. No snarky response. No attitude.

I leaned over to inhale the soup's fragrant steam. "You're not going to argue with me?"

Her smile grew. "Now that I know you look at me more like a partner and not a helpless female, I don't feel the need to snap at you."

"Ah, a shame. I sort of miss it."

She let out a soft tinkling laugh and settled back on her haunches. Withdrawing the stick she was using to stir, she set it down on a clean leaf before folding her hands over her knees and resting her chin there.

I wanted to say something about last night, but I found myself without words for it. I had been worried she'd be uneasy this morning. Scared. Angry. Maybe regretful, but instead she seemed relaxed.

I could still taste her on my tongue, and I'd woken up with a semi-hard cock. It hadn't softened at all, especially because I now sat so close to her, but at least it hadn't hardened to the painful point it had yesterday.

Bowing my head, I tried not to think about the feel of her hands on my shaft, and the sound of her moans as she came on her own fingers. But that was all that was on my mind, playing behind my eyelids on a loop. Was it because the mating bond had started? She didn't want a mate, and I didn't either, so all I had to do was avoid physical contact with her... and I could *not* kill that Joktal who had struck her.

"Are you okay with yesterday?" Her voice cut in my thoughts.

I lifted my head with a jerk. "Yesterday?"

Her head slowly turned to face me. "Yeah."

The intensity of her gaze made me feel like a bug. "I am. I'm sorry you had to help me."

"I guess we got a little carried away." She brushed off imaginary dirt from her pants. "That's normal."

"Did you have any pain?"

Her mouth opened, but it took a moment for her to respond. "Interestingly, no."

"So, skin to skin contact doesn't always cause you pain?"

"I don't know." She nibbled her lip. "Usually it does. It's

not consistent, but often, if I initiate the contact, the pain is delayed. Yesterday was... an anomaly. I've never been pain-free that long while touching someone."

"You were willing to risk it though. For me."

She smiled. "I was."

We ate after that, taking turns drinking the soup out of the pot. When the pot was empty, I sat back and wiped my face with the back of my hand. "Thank you. That was very good."

"Best I could do on short notice. What do you eat at the camp?"

"We have a few cooks, mostly the younger Drixonians. There's one named Trapt who I know wants to be a warrior, and he will be one day, but he's also a great cook, so I put him in the kitchen a lot. He makes stews and even some sweets if he's feeling nice."

"I'll meet him?"

I nodded. "You'll meet them all, including Amber and Tasha. And then we'll find the rest of your friends."

She reached for me, and her fingers trembled slightly before she lightly brushed the back of my hand. "Thank you."

I decided in quiet moments like this, with the sun streaming through the windows of the small cabin, that I liked the soft Trix without the attitude.

She pulled back her hand and began to tidy up. "We should probably move on today, right?"

"Yes, stopping here maybe wasn't the wisest decision—"

"But I think it was necessary." She pursed her lips and turned to me with raised eyebrows. "Don't you think?"

My cora did feel lighter. I no longer felt like every heart-beat was gushing blood through all of its cracks. One last thing I had to do before we left was tackle the chest in the corner.

While Tasha finished disposing of the evidence of our meal—we didn't want to attract predators—I slid the family chest into the center of the cabin. When I unlatched it, I let out a long exhale. Vivi's doll stared back at me with its black pebble eyes. I had retrieved those for her from a nearby stream. I could still remember spying them through the rippling water and splashing triumphantly to my older sister, Bemi, with the treasured rocks. She'd made the doll for Vivi, who ended up not having much time to enjoy it.

Trix couched next to me but didn't speak, and I appreciated the silence. I pulled out the doll and ran my fingers over the strips making up its hair. The fabric nearly disintegrated in my hand, and I quickly set the doll aside.

Inside were more rocks with drawings made by Bemi, along with some clothes which were stained and covered in holes and stains from vermin and age. I found a slingshot I'd made myself and had used it to scare briggers until my mother taught me to respect the species we shared the planet with.

My hands closed around a familiar set of smooth stones, and I withdrew a necklace I'd made for my mother just before she'd contracted the virus. I'd picked the stones from a cave myself and polished them with sand and water until they shone. The band was a thick piece of gamphor vine that dried into a flexible rope. Even after all these cycles, it had held.

"That's so pretty," Trix said, her finger grazing one of the stones. "Who did it belong to?"

"My mother. I made it for her, and would have burned it with her body, but she made me promise I'd save it."

"Why?"

"She wanted me to wear it. She believed the stones had luck left in them for someone else. But it was too big for my wrist then. I don't remember keeping it in this chest, but I guess I saved it here."

I turned and slid the stone bracelet onto Trix's wrist, careful not to touch her skin.

Her eyes lifted to mine. "I—I don't think I should wear it."

The sight of it on her wrist did something funny to my chest. I could still picture the beads on my mother's thicker arm. I couldn't describe why I felt so strongly about this, but I knew that Trix needed to own this. "I gifted it to you. It's yours now."

"Kutzal," she whispered.

I stood up and closed the trunk before pushing it back in its place. She remained crouched where she was, but I walked past her.

"Kutzal," she said again as she rose to her feet.

I whirled around, pointed a finger at her, and said the first thing I could on my mind. "I want you to wear it."

She jerked back at my sharp tone. Then she let out a huff and propped her hands on her hips. "Fine," she said. "But in the future, let's discuss the proper way to give someone something. Barking at them about it isn't quite in line with the gift-giving spirit is all I'm saying."

I turned around with a smile on my face. She still had her attitude. And I still liked it.

We stopped at the nearby stream to fill our qua skins and then headed off in the direction of the Lone Howl camp. I told Trix I wanted to cover as much distance as possible, and she agreed. "I'm ready to see the girls," she'd said with a tough jut of her chin.

She kept pace with me, which didn't surprise me. Trix was a tough human, and I was proud to have her at my side. I hadn't been lying when I told her I viewed her on the level of my warriors. No matter what happened, for the rest of my life I'd protect this female. I worried how much she was getting under my skin, but promised that once we got to camp, she'd be busy with Amber and Tasha. We'd have distance between us, and that was a good thing. Right?

As we walked, the silence of the forest seemed almost... too quiet. I kept looking for Joktal tracks and listening for the braying of their hounds, but only an eerie silence and the rustling of our own footsteps could be heard.

I didn't even see much wildlife. Trix seemed on alert too, her sweaty brow furrowed as her gaze constantly darted around to take in our surroundings.

We rested that night only briefly and were on the move again before the sun rose. And still... that eeriness pervaded. At one point, Trix and I made eye contact, and I caught a sliver of fear hiding in her green gaze. My scales prickled, and I had to force myself not to raise my machets as a creeping dread soured my stomach.

Suddenly, Trix lightly smacked my shoulder and pointed in the distance. Barely detectable was a thin plume of gray smoke wafting up between the trees. It didn't smell like a wood-fire. It smelled... mechanical. My gut churning, I signaled for her keep the noise down as we made our way toward the smoke plume.

As we drew closer, evidence of a crash could be seen. Brush was trampled and burned while a few tree trunks had been notched out with something hard and jagged.

When I caught sight of a familiar hunk of metal, my

stomach plummeted into my feet. I motioned for Trix to remain where she was as I unleashed my machets and stalked forward slowly.

A familiar boot came into view, as well as a blue arm, and as much as I wanted to rush to my warrior's side, I had to be cautious. What if this was a trap? I listened for breathing other than my own and Trix's. I tossed a rock at the crashed hover bike where it plunked off the handlebars and thunked to the ground. The arm didn't move at the sound, and my cora pounded.

"Fleck it," I murmured to myself and crept closer. My gaze traveled up the arm, noting the coating of black blood on the warrior's shoulder, before my eyes landed on a face I knew all too well.

"Trapt!" I shouted as I lurched toward the crash site. Sliding to my knees at his side, I took in the warrior's wounded body. Trix ignored my orders and came rushing to my side. She clapped her hands over her mouth at the sight of my youngest warrior lying motionless on the ground. Her eyes immediately filled. "Is he...?"

Bending down, I held my ear above his parted lips. When I felt the softest, lightest, barely there puff of air, I nearly collapsed. "He's alive. But I don't know for how long."

I tried to assess what happened but could only determine that Trapt had crashed his bike. He was an accomplished rider, like all of us were, so that didn't make sense.

Trix was already on her knees wetting some spare cloth and swiping at his injuries. As she wiped away the blood, I was able to see better how he'd been injured, and his wounds weren't all indicative of a crash.

I rolled his shoulder to check under him and sure enough, an arrow lay bent beneath this body while the point remained embedded in his back. I slowly withdrew it from his body and pressed on the wound to stem the bleeding. When I held the arrow up to Trix, her eyes narrowed. "Joktals."

"I can't understand why he's here and not at camp. Why would he leave?"

"Was he looking for you?"

I shook my head. "I left Lukent in charge. He'd never authorize Trapt to search for me on his own. And Trapt wouldn't disobey an order." I swiped at a smear of blood his cheek as my throat tightened. "He's a good one." His chest hitched, and he let out a muted moan as his eyelids fluttered. I glanced up at Trix. "We have to get him back to camp so the healer can tend to him."

"Of course," she nodded, eyes wide as sweat beaded on her forehead.

Trapt let out another moan, and I could have sworn he said no. "Trapt?" I turned my head, so his hot breath tickled my ear. "What is it?"

His hands flailed before finding purchase on my arm. His fingers squeezed my scales as a low, pained tone rumbled from his lips. "Can't... go."

"Can't go where?"

His eyes opened a crack, the violet rimmed in streaks of red. "Camp. Need... help."

My cora beat a rapid flurry in my chest. I shouldn't have ignored the sense of foreboding...

"What do you mean they need help? What happened?"

"Joktals," he whispered. "Surrounded."

"Oh my God," Trix's hand pressed against her mouth.

"Siege," he continued. "Waiting for... you." He groaned as he shifted in my arms. His tongue snuck out to lick his cracked lips. A bit more awareness came back into his eyes, but his expression remained tight with pain. "Camp is under siege. No one hurt yet. Females protected. Lukent sent me to Granit but Joktals crashed me." His breath shuddered out. "Didn't even try to play dead. Thought I was dead 'til I heard your voice." His head lolled on his neck. "Sorry, drexel. I failed."

Trix let out a short sob from behind her hand. Watery eyes swirling with concern and anger met mine.

Draped over my leg, Trapt's hair once shiny hair hung limp and knotted with leaves and matted with blood. I smoothed the locks off his forehead as my blood heated to a rolling boil. Trapt had always been like a younger brother to me. Sometimes even a son. I'd kept him protected from a lot of the violence as the Uldani had treated him like garbage. But to me, he was one of the best of us.

"You didn't fail," I gutted out through clenched teeth. "You're alive. That's what matters to me." I turned to Trix. "I need you to stay with him."

Her eyebrows furrowed. "I'm sorry?"

"They think he's dead, so you'll be safe."

"And where are you going to be?"

"I'm going to camp to end this siege—"

"No!" Trapt rasped with a hoarse shout. "That's too many."

I looked down at him with a snarl. "I can take them on—"

"Are you crazy?" Trix hissed at me. "No way are you taking on an army of Joktals with their nose hounds by yourself."

"They have my warriors pinned—"

"And your warriors aren't waiting for you and only you to save the day," she spat at me. "I know you have taken on the burden of their survival on your own, but this is the time to ask for *help*, Kutzal." Her tone softened somewhat. "You're not thinking clearly, and I get it. I want to stomp in there and get my girls, but it's a suicide mission. We have to go to Granit. Trapt can get treated there, and we can ask Daz for help."

She was right, I knew she was right. Informing Daz of the threats to us and keeping his warriors on standby had been one thing—it was in his interest to contain the threat before it reached his family. But this felt...different. This was asking him to risk his warriors to save mine. The expendable clavas. The outcasts. The sons of naught. The nothings.

What if I arrived there and he said he couldn't send anyone? I wasn't sure I'd be able to take it.

"I'll be there with you." Trix's tentative touch settled on my neck, and her thumb rubbed the sharp point of my jaw. "I'll fight with you. We have to do everything in our power to save them." I leaned into her fingers, and she smiled, her eyes blurry with tears. The bracelet on her wrist sparkled in the sun. "Let's ask for help," she said. "What will I do if something happens to my drexel?" A small smile curled her lips. "It's no fun fighting without you by my side."

Trapt coughed weakly in my arms, and I curled my arms around him tighter. With a nod, I met Trix's eyes. "Then let's get going to Granit."

She grinned in triumph.

EIGHT

Trix

I could feel the simmering panic underneath Kutzal's stoic exterior. Carrying a half-conscious Trapt on his back, Kutzal weaved around trees, sped across meadows, and splashed through streams with a single-minded focus. Sometimes when Trapt would moan in pain, Kutzal would murmur some reassuring words to him, but other than that, he rarely spoke.

I just tried my best to keep up. He moved at a blistering pace and while I was in shape, the journey was taxing on my body. I scooped water in my skin on the go and snatched berries off trees as we passed them. I didn't dare ask Kutzal to stop, and truthfully, I didn't *want* to stop. Kutzal wasn't the only one with the lives of loved ones on his shoulders. Trapt wasn't able to give us much more information as he seemed nearly delirious. While his flesh wounds had already begun healing, I worried about any internal wounds and a possible head injury or an infection. Did Drixonians even get infections, and would they have antibiotics at this Granit city?

The questions and the anxiety swirled in my mind and gut until I was nearly sick with it. My stomach stopped wanting food and instead cramped up every time I tried to swallow something. I kept my bow and arrow poised in case we were ambushed as Kutzal was hindered by carrying the injured Trapt.

Between running with Kutzal and staying alert for enemies, exhaustion soon set in. But I refused to stop. I refused to hold us up. Kutzal seemed in a trance, running with sure steps and dull eyes.

We reached a line of trees, and I caught sight of a light blinking somewhere in the trees. I tried to call out to Kutzal to alert him, but my voice came out in a weak croak. Kutzal raced beyond the line of trees and slowly came to a stop. Panting, he stood in place, Trapt loosely wrapped around his back, and tilted his head back to the sky. I stumbled to his side, pitching forward to brace my hands on my knees as I fought to stay upright. How long had we ran? A full day? A day and a half? I vaguely remembered a night sky at one point. But the sun was out now, beating down on my skin through the large leaves overhead.

A dull buzzing reached my ears, and I swayed closer to Kutzal. "Wha—?" I licked my dry lips. "What's that sound?"

Kutzal breathed heavily, and before he could answer, Trapt's voice mumbled in a low rasp. "Help."

"*Help?*" The air seemed to shimmer, and the buzzing drew closer. It was then I recognized the sound. I'd heard it the first time I met Kutzal when he'd flown to a stop on his massive hover bike.

This sound was multiplied, sounding like a hive of bees, then the roar of Harley Davidsons, and then like a tornado as the trees seemed to bow inward just as a set of two bikes shot between the tall branches. Four more followed, and then maybe a half dozen after that. In a V-formation, they settled to a stop in front of us. One of the Drixonians—a tall warrior with a long braid and pierced nipples—hopped off his bike and approached quickly, his face etched in concern as he took in our condition. I could only imagine how I looked—dirty, sweaty, and near death. Trapt's eyes were closed, his head lolling on Kutzal's shoulder and Kutzal... well, Kutzal looked a second away from losing his ever-loving mind. His jaw was tight enough to crack a fang, and every muscle in his body bulged with the effort of our journey.

"Kutzal," the braided Drix said as his eyes took in the three of us. His gaze lingered on me, and his eyes tightened. "What happened?"

"Long story." Kutzal winced as the braided Drix eased Trapt off his shoulders. He stretched out his arms with a grimace. "I need to talk to Daz. Trapt needs help, and the female needs to see a healer."

"I'm fine," I murmured, but my voice didn't sound fine. In fact, it sounded underwater. But I was standing on land, so that didn't make sense. My vision went fuzzy at the edges as I blinked sweat out of my eyes.

"Fleck, she's dead on her feet," growled a different voice. I lifted my head and squinted to see who spoke. Something on his head caught my attention. "Do—do you have a mohawk?" I let out a hiccup that turned into a wheezing laugh. "Well, shit. You got pomade here?" I continued to laugh as the sea of Drixonians in front of me turned into one blue blur.

A hand reached for me—I think it was the mohawk one —and I jerked back with a cry to avoid the inevitable pain. Suddenly a big body slipped in front of me, blocking out my visions, and I inhaled Kutzal's familiar scent.

"Don't touch her," he growled.

"She was about to fall—"

"I know, and I have her. Only me. She can't—" he let out a low growl. "Just don't touch her."

I felt a weird sob bubble up my throat. I was going to pass out. Or throw up. Or both. "Trix," his voice rumbled. "Touch me first. Touch me now so I can touch you."

Reaching out, I curled my fingers around his waist, and his body went tight. "Please," I whispered. "Please help."

Familiar arms wrapped around me just as my head tilted back, shouts of alarm rose around me, and the world went black.

Pain shot through my arm, and I cried out. My eyes wouldn't open no matter how hard I tried. Where was I? Someone was touching me. I could feel their fingers on the inside of my wrist.

"I'm just taking her pulse."

"You're hurting her," a deep voice growled from a short distance. I knew that voice. Kutzal. That was Kutzal."

"Ku—" I tried to make my swollen lips move. The pain was nearly unbearable. The fingers keep pressing, *pressing*. "Kutz—"

"I tried to keep him out, Val," said another voice I recognized. The braided Drix. "But he's a surly bastard."

"I can't treat her if he's—"

"You can't treat her by touching her!" Kutzal roared.

"Kutzal," I sobbed and opened my eyes a crack to see him wrestling with the braided and mohawked Drix a few feet away from where I lay. I tried to swipe at whoever was touching me, but my arms felt too heavy to move. Weak and helpless, I could only plead for Kutzal from my prone position. "*Help.*"

"Let go!" Kutzal's muscles bulged, and he thrust his arms back, dislodging the two Drix holding him. He rushed to my side just as the painful touch stealing my breath abated. He didn't touch me, only caged me with the wide span of his arms and turned his head to snarl. "I said, you're *hurting her.*"

Finally free from pain, I took in my surroundings. The room was fairly plain with a series of cabinets lining the walls, wheeled trays, and a row of cots. I lay on one, a blanket pulled up to my chest. I fingered the cloth to find it was soft and pleasing to the touch. Standing next to my head, staring at me with wide, alarmed eyes, was a human woman wearing a simple pair of pants and a long-sleeved shirt.

A human woman.

I blinked at her, she blinked back before turning her lips up in a tentative smile. "Hello, I'm Val."

I didn't know what to say, so I only stared back at her. Why was there a human woman here?

The braided Drix stepped to her side and pushed her slightly behind him as he glared at Kutzal. "Yell at my mate again, and I'll break your horns off and stab you with them."

Kutzal bared his teeth. "I'd like to see you try, Sax."

"Stop," Val said to her mate. I noticed the matching marks on their wrists. Loks, Kutzal had called them. But I still didn't understand...

"Why is there a human here?" I whispered.

Kutzal's expression softened as he looked down at me. "Because many of the warriors here are mated to human females they rescued."

"There are more..." I lifted my hand to my aching head and took a deep, calming breath. "You didn't think to tell me that?"

"It didn't come up." He sounded petulant.

I squinted at him. "It didn't come up?"

"It wasn't like we planned to come here. And then I sort of... forgot."

"You forgot."

"Um, excuse me," Val pushed her mate slightly, but he didn't budge. He'd stopped glaring at least, and his gaze bounced between Kutzal and me. "I can explain everything once I get you checked out. Kutzal said your name is Trix?"

I nodded dumbly, still amazed to see a human woman, who was clean, plump, and seemed happy.

"You're very dehydrated." Her hand reached for me. "So, if I could just get this IV in you—"

I jerked away from her so hard that I would have fallen off the bed if it wasn't for Kutzal's body blocking the way. My chest heaved as Val froze, her hand hovering in the air. Confusion marred her pretty features. "Do you... not want the IV?"

"Please no," I whispered.

"I told you all repeatedly." Kutzal curbed his tone only slightly. "Don't touch her."

"Why not?" Sax snapped.

"Sax, please. I can handle this." Val gave him a tight smile. "Trix, that's fine. I don't have to touch you. But I need you to drink and eat."

"Give it to me." Kutzal planted his ass on the side of the bed near my shoulder. "I'll help her."

"I can feed myself."

I reached for a water cup on the table near my head, but I misjudged the distance and instead smacked it off the table. It hit the floor and splashed water all over Val's shoes.

"Shit," I winced. "I'm sorry."

"I'll take care of her." Kutzal's voice was firm. A decision meant to be obeyed.

Val's eyes met mine. "Is that okay?"

"Yes, please."

She smiled. "Great. We'll get you some fortified water and quick protein. You're likely anemic so I have some iron supplements as well."

"I'm sorry." Kutzal lifted a spoon to my lips. I opened my mouth, and he slipped the cooled porridge into my mouth. The taste was sweet, a bit like maple-syrup flavored oatmeal, although the texture was a little off. Val said it was her special concoction and I truly didn't ask what the ingredients were. I was already feeling stronger. I didn't tell Kutzal that though. I kind of liked him feeding me. I lay against him in the crook of his arm while he fed me. My skin remained warm and pain-free from his touch.

"Sorry for what?" I said around my mouthful of porridge.

"I should have been more attentive to you. I was so focused on getting to Granit..." He shook his head, clearly angry with himself.

"Hey," I brushed my fingers along his thigh. "I could have spoken up. I wanted to get here as fast as you did." I swallowed and craned my neck to look him in the eye. "How's Trapt?"

Kutzal pointed to a bed at the far end of the room, where I could see Trapt's feet hanging over the edge of a cot. Val stood over him, talking softly. "He's doing all right. Some broken bones that we're trying to get mended properly before they heal incorrectly."

"But he's okay? He'll live?"

Kutzal nodded. "He'll live. And thrive. Now focus on eating."

A few minutes later, and he was scraping the bowl with the spoon while I rubbed my full stomach. Val had placed a pitcher of water near me and instructed me to drink it all slowly. I took a few careful sips and then placed it back on the table. I looked at my hands which were streaked with dirt and covered in scratches and dried blood. "Is there somewhere I can get clean?"

He frowned. "You need to stay in bed."

"I can't lay here a minute longer in my own filth, Kutzal. Please."

He sighed. "I guess we could both use the cleanser." He helped me up, and once he made sure that I could stand on my own two feet without falling over, he led me to the back of the room. My gaze drifted to Trapt, who was sleeping. As we walked past his bed, Val turned to us and smiled.

After the scene we'd made, I felt a little guilty. "I'd like to start over between us, if that's okay."

Her laugh was light. "Of course."

"I'm sorry for—"

"Don't apologize," she waved a hand. "I should apologize for touching you without your permission. But you were in such bad shape and the only thing on my mind was getting fluids in you. You look much better now that you've eaten and hydrated."

"I feel a lot better." I gestured to the slender doors at the back of the room. "Kutzal said we can use the cleansers?" While I hadn't used a cleanser in a long time, I had used them when I'd been held by the Uldani.

"Yes, of course. I'm sure you want to get clean. Will you be all right?"

"I will."

"I'll get you a change of clothes and place fresh bedding on your bed."

Both those things sounded heavenly. I smiled at her gratefully. "Thank you."

While Kutzal retreated to his own cleanser, I stepped into my own stall and removed my clothes. A shower hung from the wall, and when I pressed the button nearby, a powerful stream of filtered air streamed down, stripping my hair of oil and cleansing my skin of dirt and filth. I closed my eyes, breathing in the fresh air until the timer was up. I glanced down at my bare feet and wiggled my toes. Blisters covered my soles and heels, and I knew I'd have to give them a break before I could slip back into my boots.

When I turned to the door, a set of clothes hung over the top of the door, and I unfolded them to take a look. The pants were wide and loose with a drawstring waist and the shirt was oversized and hung off one shoulder. She even supplied a homemade bra with a reed support which was better than the band I'd been wearing across my chest. I padded out in my bare feet, feeling more like myself than I had in ages.

Kutzal stood in the center of the room wearing a clean pair of pants and nothing else. His shiny hair hung down to the center of his back. He turned at the sound of my footsteps, and his eyes softened as he took me in. "Feel better?"

"Much," I agreed. My legs were still a little wobbly, and I was already thirsty again.

Val gestured to my bed, which now bore new, clean sheets. "I can't thank you enough." I sank into bed and pulled the soft blanket into my lap. "I am sorry for reacting so badly to you."

"I meant it when I said you don't need to apologize."

"Is Sax... your mate... angry at us?"

She smiled. "Don't worry about him. He's probably forgotten all about it."

Kutzal snorted. "Not likely." He sat down in a chair near my bed and handed me a cup of water. "Drink."

I took a few gulps while Val stood nearby organizing a tray of instruments. "So, are there more of us here?" I asked her.

"Humans?"

I nodded.

She smiled. "Yes, quite a few. About a dozen. Many of us have children too."

My eyes nearly bugged out. "Children?"

"Sax and I have a son."

"How long have you been in this galaxy?"

She tapped a finger to her lips as she thought. "I'm not sure. Maybe five to six years? Most of us were rescued by the Drixonians before we could be sold to the Uldani and lived on Torin until we all migrated here to Corin."

I felt Kutzal's hand brush my thigh in a comforting touch. "I see," I murmured. So, she was a lucky one, saved before being sent to the Uldani. "Well, life with the Uldani wasn't fun, so I'm glad you avoided that."

I expected her to smile, but instead her eyes went a little distant. "I was not one of the ones rescued first. I spent time with the Uldani. Underground." I knew the surprise showed in my face when her eyes held mine. Did she know... about me?

"I met Tasha." She went on. "Kutzal said she's your friend?"

I sat up. "You met Tasha? We were separated before any of us met the Drixonians."

She nodded. "She came here with her mate, Lukent. He was very sweet to her." She stepped forward and seemed to reach to pat my hand before thinking better of it. "You'll meet your friends again. I know you will."

The door opened, cutting short our conversation, and a large Drixonian stepped through. His long hair hung in around his shoulders in a shiny sheet like a shampoo commercial. Wicked horns curled out of his temples, and he wore a large septum ring. His eyes were a piercing violet, and his presence was... overwhelming. Commanding. I forced myself not to shrink back into Kutzal even though I wanted to. Val retreated to the back of the room to makes notes at a small desk.

Kutzal jerked at the sight of this Drixonian, and slowly stood. His hands crossed at the wrist in front of his neck, and he murmured in a deep, reverent voice, "Hello, drexel. I'm sorry I haven't come to see you yet."

The big warrior shook his head. "You were attending to the female, which is important, so I came to you."

Kutzal nodded before dropping his hands and once again sank down into the chair next to my bed. He kept his gaze on the big warrior.

"I'm Dazeem Bakut," said the big warrior. "I'm sorry we are meeting in these circumstances."

"Trix," I said with a shaky voice. "My name is Trix."

"I met Lukent's mate, Tasha. I understand she's a friend?"

I nodded quickly. "Yes. I-I have been trying to find her, as well as the others."

Daz's gaze swung to Kutzal. "Tell me what's happened."

NINE

KUTZAL

I didn't leave anything out. Daz had to know the Joktals weren't above using the females as bait.

"She shot you?" Daz's lips twitched and I didn't bother to hide my glare.

"I feel bad about it now," Trix said. "But at the time I was doing what I thought was right."

I shrugged. "I was impressed. It was a good shot."

Daz nodded. "Go on."

I let him know what the Upreth planned to do with me, and how we escaped. "Trapt said the Lone Howl camp is under siege, and Lukent sent him to ride here to Granit to ask for your help, but the Joktals intercepted him and crashed his bike. They thought he was dead." I glanced over to see Trapt flat on his back, eyes closed, breath whistling through his teeth as he slept deeply. His tail twitched as it hung off the side of the bed.

I rubbed my hands together as I eyed Daz. Trix seemed

to sense what I was about to say and gave me a reassuring nod. "I need help ending the siege. I know we are sons of naught, but we have females there now, human females with cora eternal Drix mates, so I hope that warrants receiving aid for the siege." I bit my tongue as I waited for his response.

Daz leaned back in his chair with his arms crossed over his muscled chest. His mouth went tight, and his eyes flashed with irritation. "When Lukent came to me and asked for help finding the rest of the human females, the only reason I didn't immediately send a fleet of warriors was because I didn't want to risk a large-scale war. But we are now past that. The Joktals have made the first move, and now it's imperative we defend ourselves." He leaned forward in his chair and his piercing eyes held mine. "My decisions had nothing to do with you being sons of naught. You are Drixonian warriors. And in my eyes, every warrior is worth saving. Do you understand me?"

My cora beat against my chest, and an odd lightness spread throughout my limbs. I didn't know what to do or what to say, so I finally decided to croak out, "I understand."

"We will end this siege and save the Lone Howl camp under one condition," Daz said.

I sucked in a breath, unable to hide my reaction. I straightened my back as Trix's fingers tightened on the blanket. "What condition?" I asked.

"You move camps closer to Granit."

I was sure the shock of my statement registered all over my face. "Move?"

He rubbed at the nubs on his brow as he grumbled. "Frankie told me I need to explain myself, so I'm going to try." He heaved out a breath. "I was content to let you set up camp on our borders. The Lone Howl clavas is full of excellent trackers and scouts. And to be frank, I wanted to respect you as drexel, Kutzal. I know you're protective of your warriors and enjoyed the seclusion. But I'm pulling rank now. Move to a village close to Granit. The one we moved from is vacant now, and you can live there. You're a Drixonian, Kutzal." Daz's jaw clenched as his eyes fired. "As long as I live, I'll never brand another warrior for his father's crimes."

A strange sound rose up my throat, and I covered it before it could leave my lips with a hand over my mouth. I didn't know where to look. Daz's gaze was so intense, I could barely stand it. Tears streamed down Trix's cheeks as she made muffled sounds behind the blanket pressed to her face.

I gazed down at my clasped hands between my knees as my mother's blurred face floated across my vision. The brand on the back of my neck burned like the day I got it, and I scratched at it as my breath hitched in my chest.

"Fleck," Daz murmured quietly. "Did I mess this up?"

I shook my head and tried to speak but the words jammed in my throat. "No," I barked out, louder than I intended to. I forced myself to stay calm. "You didn't mess anything up." I met his gaze. "Thank you, Daz. I accept those conditions."

He nodded and slapped his palms on his knees. The tension in the air snapped at the sharp sound. "Great, then it's decided. You'll leave tomorrow. Tonight, you'll eat and rest. I'll take care of preparing my warriors. I need to know everything you know about the Joktals."

Trix swiped at her face. "I can help with that too. I was inside Joktalis."

"You were?" I asked.

She raised an eyebrow at me. "You weren't the only one in their cage."

I turned to Daz. "We'll tell you everything. Give me a dozen warriors and I'm confident we can beat them."

Daz gave me a chilling smile. "That, I can do." He rose to his feet. "Trix, my mate can get you set up in a room to wait for the warriors to return."

I bristled, but Trix was faster than me. "I'm sorry, what?"

Daz frowned. "You are welcome at Granit while—"

"No, no," she cut him off and swung her feet over the side of the bed. I reached to help her, but she waved me off. "I'm not waiting here."

Daz's gaze swung from her to me and then back again. "Where will you go?"

She stood and propped a hand on a jutted-out hip. "I'm going with them. Now where's my bow and arrow?"

Trix

Daz stared at me. I stared back. I could tell he was warring with himself. He wanted to remain respectful of me, but he clearly disagreed with my decision.

He tried a different track. "The Joktals are—"

"I know," I said. "I know exactly who and what they are. But I'm a good shot with an arrow, and there is no way I'm staying behind." I whirled on Kutzal, who had remained quiet during this exchange. He met my eyes steadily. For a moment, my confidence faltered. Would he back me up on this or insist I stay locked in this city like a damsel in distress? He said he viewed me as a part of his clavas... but did he really?

"Kutzal?" I queried and cringed at the wobble in my voice.

He hesitated a beat before lifting his eyes to Daz. "She will come."

My shoulders sagged with relief while Daz tensed up. "Why?"

"You heard her. She's a good shot, and she knows how to hunt. She's as invested in ending this siege as I am. She's loyal to her friends, and I respect that."

His words sent a warm flush up my neck. "Thank you," I said to him softly.

He nodded at me, but then stood so he was even with Daz. "I'll move to your village close by, but Trix comes with me."

A scuffling could be heard outside the door, and Val stood from her desk with a roll of her eyes. "If you don't let them in, they're going to end up breaking down the door."

"Who?" I asked.

Daz sighed and voices filtered through the door—several high-pitched ones followed by one deep voice. He walked quietly toward the door before resting his hand on the doorknob. He held up his hand and curled a finger one-by-one into his palm. When he made a fist, he swung the door open with a jerk.

A pile of bodies rushed through. A Drixonian warrior landed flat on his stomach while several human females flopped onto his back. Daz stood above them with a suffering look as they scrambled to their feet.

"How long were you out there?" he asked.

A short white woman with long dark hair, big brown

eyes, and freckles shot him a ferocious glare. "Why was the door locked?"

"Because I needed to talk to Kutzal, and I knew you wouldn't be able to help yourself."

Behind her stood a tall black woman with braids who was busy fixing the clothes of the other woman who had fallen through the door—she was white with dark purple hair and an ornate necklace. What caught my eye was that on each of their wrists was what looked like a golden tattooed bracelet, all in different patterns. Except the short woman's matched Daz's. These were all mated women. And they were... happy.

The warrior who'd fallen through the door reminded me of Trapt—he seemed younger with unlined skin and a kind, open smile. He reached into a sack that was slung over his shoulder and pulled out a familiar weapon.

I let out a gasp of delight. "My bow!" I reached for it and cradled it to my chest. It was crude and a little ugly. but it was *mine*. I knew it like I knew myself. I had worried they'd throw it away, thinking it was trash.

"You were low on arrows." The warrior's voice was kind and he gave me a wide smile. "I made you some more. I hope I replicated them well."

He handed me the sack, and I peered inside. Sure enough, only about half a dozen of my own arrows were inside, but there were about two dozen more, freshly made. I pulled one out and ran my fingers down the shaft. He'd cut the wood down to the same thickness of my other arrows and he'd even notched my symbol at the end—a five-pointed leaf.

My eyes went misty, and I blinked back the tears of gratitude. "I don't know what to say. These are perfect, and this is so kind. Thank you."

He beamed brightly, and the purple-haired woman held up her hand. He slapped her high-five in a human-like gesture that was funny to see in a warrior. "I'm Hap," he said. "I like to make things."

"He's so talented," piped up the purple-haired woman. "He can make anything you want. A bed, a doll, a chair, you name it."

I smiled. "That's good to know. I'm sure you're proud of your mate."

She laughed as she locked arms with Hap. "Oh, he's not my mate. He's my best friend. I'm Tabitha. My mate is Xavy, the one with the mohawk who makes moonshine."

"Maybe we shouldn't lead with the moonshine," Daz said under his breath.

"I'm Miranda," the black woman said. "You probably haven't met Drak yet, but he's my mate."

"Nice to meet you."

"And I'm Daz's mate, Frankie," the short one said. She took a step toward me as if to hug me, and I took a step back on instinct. Val sucked in a breath behind me, and Frankie's gaze swung to her before she stopped short and ducked her head. "Shit, sorry. I forgot." She offered me a smile. "I respect no hugging."

"Frankie's love language is definitely physical affection," Miranda squeezed her friend's shoulder.

"Right, so..." Frankie circled her arms in front of her with a big smile. "Uh, air-hug to you. We're happy to have you here safe and sound!"

For some reason, the gesture pierced me right in the chest. I loved my friends, and I'd established myself a bit as their untouchable protector. These women didn't know that was my role. To them... I was just another human woman who deserved to feel safe and loved. The arrows, the introductions, the smiles—all of it was more than I could have imagined.

I circled my arms in front of me as I tried to swallow around the lump in my throat. "Air hug to you all. I'm Trix."

"We met your friend Tasha," Frankie said. "She was very nice, but I think we overwhelmed her a bit. We had a large meal in our dining hall, and it was all a bit much. After what you've been through... we thought maybe you'd want to take your meal privately. We set up a room for you." She stopped herself suddenly and then followed up with a rush of words. "But if you want company, we're more than happy to join you." She bit her lip. "We've really been trying to work on accommodating each new woman with a welcome befitting their situation. We can be a lot all at once."

Miranda nodded. "Kids. Babies. Loud talking."

The kindness was nearly overwhelming. "I-I want to meet you all but now might not be the best time. I think it's best I take an early meal with Kutzal and get some rest." Knowing Tasha and Amber were out there in danger made celebrating my safety feel hollow. "We'll be moving closer to one of the nearby villages, so once we find my friends, I'll definitely be in the mood for a big party."

Frankie's eyes went wide, and she turned to Daz. "They agreed?"

Daz smiled and draped his big arm across her shoulders. "They did, cora-eternal."

Frankie beamed and pressed her palms to her cheeks as she stepped closer to Kutzal. "That's great news. I never liked you out that far."

Kutzal blinked at her, seemingly confused. "You know... about us?"

She blinked back. "Of course. I've been telling Daz that

you need to live closer to Granit, but he didn't want to overstep, I guess."

Daz cleared his throat. "Okay, mate."

She peered up at him. "What? I'm just telling the truth."

"Yes, you are, and now we can move on."

She rolled her eyes. "Ah yes, we wouldn't want to convey too many feelings at one time. We might break the space-time continuum. Open another dimension."

I snorted a laugh, and the sound surprised me. Frankie's eyes sparkled, clearly pleased with herself at being a source of amusement. "Want to see your room? Anna and Bazel fixed it up. Kutzal, you can—"

"I will stay with Trix." Kutzal cut in with a firm voice.

Frankie paused and then she continued on. "Right, you two can stay together. The room is big. Let's get you settled and then we'll send up a sampler of our best foods. We've been working on it since you arrived."

"Well, you haven't been working on it because you're not allowed in the kitchen for at least a week after the last episode." Tabitha said to Frankie.

She narrowed her eyes at her friend. "That fruit was not expired. Did you see an expiration date stamped on it?"

"I was in the expeller for a solid day," Hap grunted.

Frankie threw up her hands. "Whatever." Her eyes slid to mine. "I didn't cook. You don't have to worry."

I shook my head. "I wasn't worried. I've eaten some questionable things and have a pretty tough stomach now."

"Well follow me, you two." I noticed her eyes dipped to my bare wrists before she shot me another smile. "Only the best for our guests."

TEN

Trix

As we walked through the main residence building of Granit, called the Hall, I was glad Frankie had given me the option of a quiet meal in my room. I hadn't been around this many people in *years*, and the noise alone was a lot to take in. The halls were bustling with warriors, humans, and little pale blue children with nubby horns.

Kutzal walked at my side and angled his body to block anyone who got a bit too close to me. I didn't even have to ask him, he just... did it. He protected me like it was second nature, all while still respecting my abilities that had kept me alive this long.

Kutzal didn't seem to like the noise ever. He seemed to blanch whenever a child shrieked and the roar of laughter from deep within a room we passed seemed to set his teeth on edge.

By the time we were shown our room and were able to shut the door behind us—Frankie assured us food would be on the way—we were exhausted. Mentally. Our room was bigger than I expected, about the size of a hotel suite, with a large bed palette, a small dining table with two chairs, and a few other furniture pieces scattered around the room. There was even a painting of a sunset on the wall near the table.

I slumped down on the bed while Kutzal collapsed in a sprawl in an upholstered chair. He rubbed his forehead. "Fleck, it's loud here."

I stared at the ceiling, covered in a mish-mash of old and new beams. The entire building was renovated, but Frankie had explained they'd tried to repurpose anything they could. "This is not a place for introverts."

"What's an introvert?" he grunted. His irritability at having to socialize made me smile.

"An introvert is someone who finds their energy drained by having to interact with people. An extrovert is the oppo-site—they gain energy from people around them." I twisted on the bed so I could see his face.

His nose and lips were all scrunched up in thought. "I don't know anyone who is an extrovert. Maybe Vinz. Since mating with Amber he's clingy. Always wants to be around me and talk." He shuddered. "It's annoying."

I rolled onto my stomach and propped my chin on my fist. "I bet you wouldn't mind if he was here being clingy now, right?"

His eyes slid to mine and went soft. "No, no. I wouldn't mind."

"I thought the same thing about my friends. We are loyal and love each other, but we'd get on each other's nerves. We'd fight. It was only natural. We weren't that big of a group but sometimes I'd just need to get away. Be on my own. That was when I'd go hunt." I sighed. "I'd give anything now to listen to Lu and Maisie bicker. I'd even handle Tasha's snoring. I'd welcome it all, every moment, if I knew they were safe."

"I feel guilty sitting here while they are likely rationing their food. We have plans in place for this, and I trust Lukent, but I still feel useless."

"We're not useless," I said. "We saved Trapt's life, and we're going to ride to camp with an army of warriors at our back." I sat up and swung my legs to my side. "What will they all think about moving?"

"Now that Vinz and Lukent are mated, the atmosphere at camp has changed. All the warriors have grown a little more protective. Amber and Tasha are well-liked. They help out around camp and tended to the wounded in our last battle." He paused and then eyed me. "The Wutarks attacked our camp before I left. And we found one of your arrows. How did they get it?"

"Those assholes. They must have stolen it."

He nodded. "Tasha and Amber recognized it when it was sticking out of Vinz's arm."

I slammed my hand on the bed. "*What?* They used it?"

"They did. I still have it at camp, by the way. I was waiting to return it to its rightful owner. I was interested in this human female with the carved arrows who Tasha and Amber spoke so highly of."

I picked at the ragged edge of the fur blanket. "They are just as brave as me."

"I will agree to that. Tasha especially had no problems telling me what she thought of me."

I grinned. "That's my girl."

"Ah, I can't wait until we get back. I imagine you two will gang up on me."

I laughed. "Who me? No, I would never be so mean."

"*Right*," he drew out the word, eyes glinting with humor. It was a good look on him, especially since he'd been tense in the infirmary.

A knock at the door ended our conversation. Kutzal opened it to reveal an older white woman and a pretty blonde woman with blue eyes. The older woman smiled at me, and the skin at the edges of her eyes creased. "Hello, I'm Anna. This is Daisy."

Daisy let go of her tray with one hand to wave enthusiastically at me. "Nice to meet you." The woman was just standing there holding a tray and she still radiated sunshine. I spotted the loks on both of their wrists. Was every female here mated?

I stood up at the edge of the bed and waved. "Hi, I'm Trix."

Kutzal took the trays from them, which brimmed with food. Anna pointed to the plates. "We have a bit of a selection for you. Sometimes we try to recreate food we ate on Earth and other times we just go with the ingredients we have and come up with something new." She peered into the room. "Is there anything else you need?"

I shook my head. "No, this is more than enough. I'm really appreciative of how welcoming everyone has been."

Anna's smile broadened. "Of course. I know it's a bit of an adjustment. Tasha said there is a small group of you who have been mostly alone for a long time. I lived with my mate for about ten years in seclusion for protection—we didn't have a clavas like this to keep us safe. I had to take the large group in small doses. Just know you're welcome anytime."

"Thank you." I clasped my hands at my chest. "If all goes well... we'll be seeing much more of each other."

"Daz is sending in Rex, Fenix, and Mikko, so..." Daisy's

eyebrows waggled. "Those Joggles won't know what hit them."

"Joktals," Anna whispered out of the corner of her mouth.

Daisy giggled. "Right, Joktals. Whatever."

"What is special about Rex, Fenix, and Mikko?" I asked.

"Rex is my mate and he's... um..." she fluttered her hands at her shoulders. "He has wings."

"Wings?" I jerked to Kutzal who watched me steadily. He gave me one nod.

"Mikko can eject his spikes like flying knives and Fenix... Fenix can lob fireballs."

"I'm sorry." My head throbbed. "Who are they? X-Men aliens?"

Daisy just smiled, unperturbed by my confusion. "No, they are Drixonians who the Uldani tried to turn into super soldiers. We call them the stolen warriors."

My knees wobbled, and I grasped at the bed behind me to keep myself upright. The tension was back in Kutzal's muscles, and his eyes remained locked on me.

"Are you okay?" Daisy's expression registered concern as she took a step inside.

"I'm fine." Get it together, Trix. "You just shocked me, is all. I know a bit about the Uldani's experiments."

Daisy nibbled her lip as she glanced at Anna. "I'm sorry."

"No, it's okay. I'm eager to meet them. Are they okay with helping us on our mission?"

"Mikko has been itching to fight for a while now," Anna said. "He's been driving us all crazy because he has too much pent-up energy. And the other two..." she looked at Daisy.

"The other two want to help," Daisy finished. "They feel invested."

Did they know? About me and Tasha and Amber? But I didn't want to talk about it. Not now. Everyone seemed to know I didn't like to be touched and respected it. I didn't need to get into the details. "Well, I will be sure to thank them."

"We'll leave you two to eat and rest then," Anna said. "We'll have a morning meal for you before you leave and will pack supplies as well."

They said their goodbyes and then closed the door behind them. I sank down in a chair at a small table after the click of the lock bolted into place. Kutzal laid the food trays on the table and sat down across from me. He folded his hands on top of the table. "Are you okay?"

"Why didn't you tell me about the stolen warriors?"

He ran a hand through his hair. "I'm sorry, Trix. I didn't know that we'd ever come here, and it wasn't like we have had that much time together to talk. I'm almost two hundred cycles old. That's a lot of history to cover."

He had a point. I wasn't upset with him for not telling me. I just hadn't liked being surprised. "Do you know these warriors?"

"I have met them briefly. Daz and his brothers—Sax and Rex—were from a prominent family before our society fell. I didn't exactly run in the same circles as him." He dipped his head to meet my eyes. "Are you angry with me?"

I shook my head. "No. I was just surprised. I didn't know if there was a reason you hadn't told me."

"No reason, other than worrying that talking about them would be too traumatic for you. You nearly collapsed when Daisy mentioned it."

He wasn't wrong. My mind was already going back

there. Imagining the cold, the smells, and the pain. I closed my eyes but snapped them open when he barked out my name.

"What?" Alarmed, I looked around the room.

He pointed a finger inches from my face. "Don't go there. I could see your eyes go vacant. You're not there. You're here. You're Trix and you're going to save your friends. Understand?"

His deep voice rattled my rib cage. Like a soldier, I nodded. "I understand."

"Now eat," he grunted as he reached for a plate. He sniffed the dish, which looked a bit like green spaghetti with meatballs. "Was is this?"

I reached for a plate that had slices of pink meat on it. "Do you know what this is?"

"Hordix," he muttered before stealing a slice and dropping it whole into his mouth. He barely chewed before swallowing.

"Did you even taste that?"

"A bit." He dug a spoon in the green pasta dish and shoveled half of it down his gullet. Again, with the no chewing.

"You're going to get a stomachache if you don't chew."

He stared at me before blatantly popping a piece of fruit between his lips and immediately swallowing. "You're not the only one with a tough stomach."

I laughed, shook my head, and dug into my own plate. I, however, *did* chew and swallow.

I snuggled down under the furs, barely able to believe I was sleeping on something clean for the first time in a long time.

The sunset picture on the wall drew my attention, as it was of Earth—the green trees, brown dirt, and lumbering bear in the corner gave it away.

I'd been surviving for so long, and I'd been so proud of what the girls and I had accomplished. But now I saw there was so much more we could be doing on this planet. Here in Granit, they weren't just surviving. They were living, expanding, and creating *art*. I had expected a bunch of posturing alpha aliens followed by meek human mates, but that wasn't the case here. It was a family. A community. The loks were seeming less and less like shackles than I thought, which made me feel conflicted.

The bed dipped beside me as Kutzal settled his bulk on top of the sheet. He'd stripped down to a pair of loose shorts that reminded me of the green Marine silkies I'd seen some guys wear at my kickboxing club. They left little to the imagination, and I tried not to stare at his obvious bulge. I wore a large T-shirt and a pair of underwear and still felt naked.

Kutzal folded his arms behind his head and blinked at the ceiling. Deep in thought, he remained silent while a muscle in his jaw ticked.

"Are you worried?" I asked.

He rolled his head to face me. "Worried?"

"About tomorrow. Riding to camp. Defeating the Joktals."

He studied my face before answering. "You don't want false reassurances, right?"

The question felt a little like a kick to the gut. "I would never admit this to anyone else, but a part of me wants you to just tell me it'll all be okay. That everyone we care about will be safe."

"And the other part of you?"

"The other part of me needs to know the reality."

He rolled onto his side and rested his palm flat on the bed between us, his little finger inches from mine. "I'm not worried, but I am also not overconfident. I will say that the addition of the stolen warriors will likely give us the upper hand. I have seen what Fenix can do from a distance and it is... devastating to enemies." He snapped his fingers. "He creates fire as easy as this and can manipulate it to fling at enemies."

"Did they escape the Uldani like us?"

He shook his head. "They were the experiments that went bad. Each of them has an enhancement but with negative side effects, so they were sold. Fenix worked the mines on Vixlicin while Rex was a gladiator."

"That's horrible."

"They didn't think they would be welcomed back. It took them meeting their mates to realize that they would always be welcome among us." He paused. "Just like you and your friends will always be welcome among the other females. You know that, right?"

"I didn't know that," I answered honestly. "But now... I'm starting to see that I would be." I swallowed. "I tried to tell myself all this time that my inability to be touched without pain wasn't a hardship. I didn't need physical affection. But seeing the way these women are so tactile with each other... it's reminding me more of what I lost."

His hand crept closer to mine, until I felt the slight brush of skin against skin. No pain flared. "Why can we touch?"

I shook my head. "I'm not sure. I've tried with the other girls plenty of times, but it was never as successful as it is with you."

His fingers lifted off the fur. "Can I?"

When I'd first met Kutzal, he'd been an enemy. His touch had pained me like everyone else. But slowly, he'd become someone I trusted as much as Tasha. He protected me, respected me, and cared for me. I could still feel the heat of his body as he'd caged me with his arms to protect me from touch, and how he'd snarled at Val to leave me alone. He'd fought two of his own warriors to get to me.

I'd trusted my girls, but they hadn't been able to touch me like Kutzal had. Maybe it was that not only did I trust him, I also felt protected. I couldn't be sure as whatever the Uldani did to me hadn't made sense. Like the stolen warriors, most of us had negative side effects of our mods as well. Kutzal was an anomaly. A curveball life threw at me that I hadn't seen coming. I didn't just want to *be touched*. I wanted *his touch*.

I nodded, and he curled his hand around mine before lacing our fingers together. A lump jammed in my throat as the warmth of his scales coated my palm. I felt no pain, only the heat of his body and the soft puffs of his breath.

"Will you...touch me more?"

I knew it was a lot to ask. Kutzal didn't want a mate, and I wasn't sure I did either. But the vivid images of that night in the cabin flashed in front of my eyes. I could still hear the raspy, lust-laced heat of his words, and I could still smell the pungent scent of my arousal as it hung in the air between us.

While his expression didn't change, his eyes reacted immediately, flaring within. He swallowed before speaking. "What are you asking of me, Trix?"

"You're going to make me spell it out?"

He nodded. "I am. I don't want there to be confusion here. It's too important."

It's too important. His words cracked open my chest like

a hammer to porcelain. This mattered to him as much as it mattered to me. How had we gotten here after all we'd been through?

"I want you to make me come," I whispered.

His breath shuddered out, and the bulge in his shorts jerked against the thin fabric. The outline of his mushroom head was visible, and a damp spot had already soaked through.

"And you want me to touch you to do it?"

I nodded.

"How Trix?" he slid a little closer until his hair tickled my skin. "How do you want me to touch you?"

"I—" I licked my dry lips. "I don't—"

"My fingers? My tongue? My cock? How do you want me to make you come?"

Holy shit, I was going to just from his voice if he kept talking. Instead, I heard myself say, "Any of it. All of it."

His nostrils flared. "I need you to promise you'll tell me if you feel any pain."

"I promise."

"I mean it, Trix."

Understanding this was important to him, I nodded solemnly. "I know. And I mean my promise."

"Let me see you first."

At the same time, we kicked off what little clothes I had on. Kutzal peeled the furs below my feet as I lay on my back. I'd never been overly self-conscious about my body, but I did think a lot about how I looked during sex. Did I have a double chin? Was my hair a mess? Were my boobs hanging weird?

But when Kutzal looked at me, I didn't feel any of those things. I only felt, desired. His eyes poured over me like he hadn't eaten for weeks and had just been served a feast.

"We'll start together," he said on a hoarse rasp. He brought our joined hands to his mouth. My middle finger rubbed along his full bottom lip before he slid it between his lips along with his. There, he sucked on them, tugging gently, nipping at the pad of my finger before rolling it over the piercing on his tongue. Then he withdrew the fingers and lowered them to my mouth. I opened immediately and sucked his finger inside of my mouth. I hollowed out my cheeks, tasting a bit of salt left over from dinner and another taste that had to be wholly Kutzal. His chest hitched, and he prodded a fang with the tip of his tongue.

He slid our wet fingers down my neck, leaving goosebumps in their wake. He circled one of my nipples, plucking it with the tip of an unsheathed claw before scraping gently down to my belly button. There, he sheathed his claws before dipping into the top of my curls framing my pussy.

"I can still taste the sweetness of your cunt on your fingers from that night in the cabin," he said in a tight voice.

"Kutzal," my hips bucked as he slid our fingers over my clit before probing at my entrance.

"I can't tell you how many times I've imagined what you feel like inside." Together, our middle fingers entered me, and I moaned softly at the intrusion. I hadn't been penetrated by anything thicker than my own finger in a long time.

With his gaze on my face and his lips peeled back almost as if he was in pain, he pressed in farther, down to his first knuckle. I shivered as my mouth went slack at the welcome fullness.

He hovered above me, his face inches from mine. His eyes glowed like embers, and I could have sworn his horns trembled slightly. His thumb prodded my clit, and my hips bucked.

His tongue snaked out of his mouth, long and pierced, before flicking at my bottom lip. Craning my neck, I wrapped my lips around the tip and sucked. He groaned loudly before smashing his mouth against mine. Heat roared through my body and my head spun. He licked into my mouth, and his piercings clacked against my teeth as he consumed me.

My hard nipples rubbed against his chest almost to the point of pain, but I knew it wasn't... *that* pain. This was the pain of wanting, of needing release, and also the act of denying myself. Drawing this out was both exhilarating and frustrating.

He pulled our fingers from my body, and my arousal dripped down my inner thighs. His hand clutched my throat, fingers squeezing my jaw, as he continued to kiss me into oblivion.

"I can smell how soaked you are," he breathed against my lips. "I need to taste the source. Smother myself in it."

"Jesus," I moaned. The dirty talk from the stoic Kutzal was unexpected.

He released my jaw and proceeded to slide down my body. When he reached my pussy, he hooked my knees over his massive shoulders and cupped my ass in his giant hands like he held a bowl of nectar and was about to pour it down his throat.

But the nectar was...me. And when Kutzal lowered his head, I became aware very quickly that he didn't intend to make this fast.

He tapped my clit with the tip of his tongue, and my body jerked. He watched me intently from between my legs. "What is this that's so sensitive?"

"My ... my clit."

"This is your pleasure bud?"

"Um, yes. There is one inside too."

He hummed against my clit, which sent a shiver up my spine. "I will attack both."

And attack was what he did. He plunged two fingers inside of me as he sucked my clit between his kiss-swollen lips. I cried out and flailed my hands. My fingers wrapped around one of his horns and his entire body shuddered when I squeezed the hard enamel, which seemed to soften with my touch.

Between his fingers and tongue, I wasn't sure anymore if I was in pain or if this was just a type of pleasure I had never felt. Thrashing my head, I thrust his face into my pussy, unable to get enough of that wicked tongue wreaking havoc on my clit and those long, thick fingers rubbing my inner walls relentlessly. My body was under siege, and it wouldn't be long before he knocked down every single wall until I was a useless mush of a human.

He moaned and groaned between my legs like a lion eating his kill. I might have shot Kutzal with an arrow, but right now he was the successful hunter enjoying his spoils between my legs. He was getting what he wanted with every lick of that talented tongue and every curl of those dexterous fingers.

An ache in my belly intensified, scaring the shit out of me. Was this it? Was the pain back? I tried to ignore it, wanting to hold out, but the throbbing turned into an acute pain. I tugged on his horns and opened my mouth to cry out when a light exploded behind my eyes. The flames of pain morphed into shocks of pure pleasure, radiating out to every limb, to every fingertip, to every single strand of hair on my head.

A roaring sound reached my ears and I realized it was me screaming and writhing on the furs like a maniac as the orgasm rocketed through my body. When the feeling faded into a soft warmth, I swore I floated on a cloud. I blinked my eyes open to find Kutzal hovering above me, a hand cupping my face and his thumb rubbing across my cheek.

His mouth opened, but I didn't hear anything. His lips moved again, and finally my senses began working again. "Trix!" he shouted, and I realized he was alarmed. His eyes were wild and unfocused. "Talk to me! Tell me where it hurts!"

ELEVEN

KUTZAL

Pure panic lit my blood. Had I killed her? Why hadn't she said anything? One minute she'd been moaning in pleasure and the next she'd screamed until her voice was hoarse.

"Trix!" I tried again as she blinked at me with vacant eyes. Her body lay splayed below me and her chest heaved with panting breaths.

Suddenly her lips stretched into a wide smile and her shoulders shook. I stared at her, unsure if this would turn into human sobbing but instead she was ... laughing?

I leaned back on my heels as she curled onto her side and laughed uproariously into her hands. I thought I saw tears too, but I couldn't be sure. Was this a breakdown? Did I need to get someone?

"Let me get Val," I went to scurry off the bed, but her hands slapped at my thigh lazily.

"No... need," she gasped, face streaked with tears but

eyes bright with mirth. "Just need... a minute." Giggles still shook her chest, and I was distracted by her full breasts. *Focus, Kutzal. She's hurt.*

"Where did I hurt you?" I demanded to know.

"You... didn't." She finally let out one long breath and flopped onto her back. "That was just my body breaking into a thousand pieces with the most intense orgasm of my life."

I frowned. "You're not hurt?"

She shook her head and gave me a wide smile. "I'm not. I promise. I just hadn't ever felt that before. Ever."

I didn't understand. "But I didn't use my cock."

Another weak laugh bubbled out of her. "The best orgasms often have nothing to do with a precious cock."

I looked down. My cock twitched as if in answer. "We would like to challenge that theory."

She squealed a laugh of delight, and I watched in shock as her body bucked with silent, body-shaking laughter. I'd never seen her like this. I hadn't realized Trix was capable of happiness like this.

When she finished laughing, her face was flushed a deep red, and her eyes glittered like gems. "Well," she said with a smirk. "Why don't we see what he's got?"

For a fleeting moment, I hesitated. I'd been running on instinct, but I hadn't ever pleasured a woman with my cock. While I was sure sinking into her tight heat would cause me immense pleasure, I wanted it to feel good for her too. No, not just good. I wanted to shatter her world. *Again.*

As she lay below me, flushed and sated, my cock once again hardened to a spike. I wrapped my fingers around the length and stroked it, remembering how it had felt to have her hand on me.

"Show me." I watched her eyes fire with heat. "Show me where you want my cock. Touch yourself so you know what's coming."

She wasn't laughing anymore. Her chest heaved, her breasts shook, and her hands swept down her stomach with a slight tremble. Biting her lip, she peered up at me as she spread her moist folds with her fingers. "Here," she whispered.

I rubbed a finger over her slick skin. "Right here. Keep your fingers there. Feel me as I enter you."

A slight whimper escaped her lips, and she bit down so hard on her lip that the skin turned white. She nodded as I guided the tip of my cock to her entrance. I breached her, and the feel of her surrounding my head took my breath away. I resisted the urge to plunge into her depths and pound away like an animal. Her fingers brushed my shaft as I slowly pressed inside, and the combination of her heat and the backs of her knuckles on my cock made my eyes roll back into my head.

My arms shook as I restrained myself, and when I was fully seated inside of Trix, I braced myself with my fists planted on either side of her head. "Do you feel me?"

Her throat bobbed as she spoke in a hoarse whisper. "Yes."

"Just me? Only me?"

"Only you."

"I feel you too, Trix. Squeezing my cock."

Her fingers flexed at the base of my shaft and my subcock began to elongate. She glanced down, and her eyes went wide. I followed her gaze to see the swollen subcock pressed against her clit.

I felt the moment the organ began to suck. Her entire

body tightened, and she threw her head back with a cry. Her body bucked, and then her inner walls rippled around me. Tight. An instinct triggered inside of me. I reared back and slammed into her so hard she slid up the bed pallet. "Yes," she hissed out between her teeth. Her fingers dug into my waist as her eyes met mine, the green in them wild and feral. "Again. Fuck me, Kutzal."

I snapped my hips again. And again. I plundered Trix like captured prey. She went wild below me, scratching and tugging on my hair and sensitive horns. I could tell the difference in her cries now. She wasn't in pain. She was in a cyclone of pleasure, and I was right there with her. My vision tunneled down to nothing but this beautiful female in the furs. Her hair spread around her in an auburn cloud and her skin marked with my mouth and hands.

"Come on my cock," I growled. "I want to see you lose it again right before I spend my release inside of you."

Her fingers dug into my neck, her mouth went slack, and then her entire body shook. She didn't make a sound as her eyes went hazy and her inner walls squeezed me so tight I had to grit my teeth.

A spark bolted down my spine and exploded in my balls as I roared my release into the room. My cock pulsed inside of her, coating her with my release until I was drained, spent, and exhausted.

My arms gave out, and I went down onto my elbows on top of her. Our chests pressed together, I touched my lips to hers, slowly, reverently, because I didn't have much coordination left to do much else. My muscles trembled, and Trix shivered below me as if she were cold.

I forced myself to roll off her and gathered a spare shirt to clean between her legs. She let me, laying like a limp doll, eyes focusing on my ministrations. When I was finished, I pulled the furs up to her chin and tucked them in around her. She watched me with a small smile. "You don't want to look at me anymore?"

"You're shivering." I focused on securing the furs to her body. "Is that tight enough? Warm yet?"

She laughed softly. "I'm not cold. I'm just ... post-coital. I don't need to be in a fur burrito."

"What?"

She wriggled out of the furs and stretched her arms toward me. "Quit worrying. I can speak up for myself. I'll let you know if I'm cold, okay?"

I slipped into the circle of her arms and rested my hand on her chest, careful not to poke her delicate skin with my horns. Her hands sifted through my hair.

"What's a burrito?" I murmured.

"Mmm, a burrito." She yawned. "I could go for one now. It's a type of food that's delicious. Spiced meat and all kinds of toppings in an edible wrapper called a tortilla."

"Edible wrapper," I echoed. "I want to try that."

"When we're settled, I'll see if the girls here have found a way to make anything resembling a tortilla, okay?"

"I would like that."

Her hands stilled. "Did you ever think we'd come this far in our relationship? I wanted to shoot you when we first met."

"You did shoot me."

"Yeah, and I wanted to shoot you *again* after that. Multiple times."

"I wanted to string you up in a tree and leave you there, but *I* have self-control."

She laughed. "I'm glad we both restrained ourselves."

We laid in silence for a while, and I wondered if I should move. "Are you okay? This is a lot of touching."

"I'm okay," she said quietly. "Very okay. Thank you for ... this."

I glanced up at her. She met my eyes before looking away quickly. I blinked, coming back into my sense a little now that I was out of the orgasm haze. What was I doing? Laying with her as if she was my mate. She was likely confused too. I shifted away from her, and she let me go. I cleared my throat. "Of course. I'm glad it was... successful."

I winced at the word, and she didn't seem to like it much either.

"Now you know," I coughed as I slid to my side of the bed. "Now you know you are capable of reaching this level with someone."

Her eyes shot to mine and held. Something simmered there. "No, now I know I can reach this level with *you*."

My mouth went dry. "Trix..."

"I know you don't want a mate, but I don't want one either. So please don't talk about what we just did like it was some sort of training exercise. Once we are settled in the new village, we can decide what boundaries we want to set on our relationship. I'll tell you now, you try to pawn me off on someone else like I'm a used car, and I'll stick an arrow somewhere very unpleasant."

The thought of her with another warrior made me grind my molars. "I have no intention of finding you a mate."

"Good," she spat.

"Great," I barked back.

We both lay there, seething, and I felt a little like we'd taken a step back in ... whatever this was. "Trix—"

She rolled over, showing me her back. "Let's get some

sleep. It'll be a long few days capped off by a battle I'm not looking forward to."

She was right. But why did I get the sense that this battle, the one between us, was going to be the hardest of my life?

About three dozen warriors from various clavases milled around the fields surrounding Granit. Some were jovial as they talked amongst themselves and other were grim-faced as they prepared for the upcoming fight.

Trix and I had met with Daz that morning to discuss everything we knew about the Joktals. I had no idea if Upreth had only his half dozen warriors or if he'd marched on the camp with an entire army. Daz had said he would do all he could.

Three dozen warriors were far more than I expected. Even a dozen Drixonian warriors on hover bikes were enough to break an army five times our size. But three dozen warriors plus the stolen warriors? My confidence in our victory rose.

Daz approached where I stood next to a new bike with Trix. My old one would have to be recovered at some point. While I was partial to it, I'd learned long ago not to become too attached to material things.

Trix stood with her bow strapped across her chest and her arrows in a sack at her back. She didn't look out of place among the warriors, and my respect for her soared. I didn't think it could get much higher. Having her at my side soothed me in a similar way to knowing that Axton had my back. While Trix wasn't like him, our strongest fighter, she was something else that settled me inside. My gaze met hers. The tension from last night was still there, simmering slightly below the surface. But we both knew what was to come was bigger than us.

Her eyes softened a fraction before her gaze traveled over my shoulder. I turned to find Daz approaching with a scarred warrior at his back—I recognized him as Gar. Some of the human females stood behind him. Rex spoke quietly with Daisy, while Mikko's mate rubbed his shoulders. Fenix clasped hands with his mate, and he bent his head so she could whisper in his ear. Guilt weighed on my chest. These warriors were risking a lot for me and my warriors.

Daz's voice drew me out of my thoughts. "They volunteered."

I blinked. "What?"

"You used to hide your thoughts better." His gaze flitted to Trix before returning to me. He gestured around us. "Everyone riding with you volunteered. Some of them are bored of construction work on Granit or hunting game. They miss battle. We're Drixonians, after all. It's in our blood."

I swallowed, not expecting that. I had wondered if Daz had to bribe them to ride and save a bunch of sons of naught.

Daz took another step toward me, and when he reached out and grasped the back of my neck my entire body flushed hot. The heat of his palm burned the scars of my brand. Our foreheads touched, and I had to lock my knees to keep them from buckling like an immature chit. This gesture was a greeting for warriors who cared about each other. I'd never in my life been the recipient from anyone other than other sons of naught.

The crowd noise dulled around us, and I wasn't sure if it was just my tunneling focus or if anyone else had noticed

Daz's action and realized the significance. This was him accepting me publicly and bringing me into the fold. I hadn't thought I needed this or wanted this, his ally ship was enough, but this gesture was more than just between us. This was an action more powerful than words which would do a lot to end the outdated sons of naught brand.

He kept his hand on the back of my neck and pulled back slightly so he could look me in the eye. "I should have spoken up when you made your camp as far away as you did. I should have made this gesture to welcome you much sooner. I apologize for that."

I tried to breathe around the tightness in my chest. "You don't have to apologize."

He tilted his head. "I've thought about it, and you might not have responded favorably at the time."

I shook my head with a small smile. "You'd be right." I resisted the urge to glance at Trix. "Things have changed since then."

His eyes glittered. "They have."

With a squeeze, he let me go and took a step back. "You're a part of us, and you always will be. Get your warriors and come home. The village is being prepared for your homecoming as we speak."

I nodded. "I'll be back."

Daz smiled at Trix. "Feel free to use all the arrows. Hap is already making some to replace what you use."

Trix beamed a genuine smile. "I won't hold back."

"See that you don't." He stepped back to where his mate stood, listening to us talk closely. She held a small child's hand and another clung to her back in a sling. She smiled at us as he looped an arm around her shoulders.

The stolen warriors said their final goodbyes to their mates and walked toward me in a group. Rex, a Drix with violet eyes and long white hair stopped in front of me. "I'm not sure we've ever talked. Nice to meet you, Kutzal."

I nodded to them. "Nice to meet you, too."

"We defer to you. This is your camp and an enemy you know more about than us. All the warriors have been informed you're the authority in this fight."

I hadn't expected that either. Rex was a Bakut, Daz and Sax's youngest brother. The deference to me was appreciated. "Thank you."

"Everyone has been briefed by Daz, but I want to make it clear... we don't ride for him. We ride because we are Drixonians." An intensity blazed in his eyes. "We ride because *She is All*."

My arms raised automatically, and I crossed my wrists in front of my neck. "*She is All*," I answered.

Rex's eyes crinkled in a half-smile. "A few warriors will follow up behind with a load of supplies for your warriors and females. They likely are existing on preserved rations."

I nodded. "Likely. We have well fortified bunkers along the cliff."

"Good." Rex opened his mouth as if to call out to the warriors gathered, but then stopped abruptly. He nodded to me. "It's your call to mount up."

Fleck, just thinking of giving commands made me ache for my Lone Howl warriors. With a lump in my throat, I called over the crowd. "Let's ride!"

A chorus of Drix rally war cries answered my order, and the air grew thick with the buzzing of the hover bikes' ignitions.

I slung my leg over the bike and shimmied in the seat. Not quite as nice as my bike, but it would do. Trix settled in front of me with her hands on the handlebars. Her hair hung in two braids on either side of her head, and the sun glinted off something shiny in between the strands. I plucked at the object, only to come away with a cut on my finger. "What—?"

"Blades in my braid," she said matter-of-factly. "It prevents anyone from pulling my hair."

I chuckled to myself. "Smart female."

"Damn right," she glanced at me over her shoulder, and I could see the battle lust brewing in her green eyes. "Hey, when all this is over, can you teach me how to drive one of these things?"

An image of her and I riding side-by-side hunting down a herd of antella crossed my mind, and my cora swelled. "Absolutely."

She grinned and then faced forward as the hover bike rose into the air. She waved to the females waiting below, while I gave Daz a one-armed farewell. He nodded, eyes tight as he watched us ride away.

Trix whooped as we rode away, and the sound made me smile. I couldn't explain how her presence made me feel. Content. Anchored. Like I was *home*.

After my mother died, I hadn't thought I would ever feel at home ever again. The cabin wasn't the same without my family. It was just a bunch of boards and things. Trix had filled it again, but it didn't matter where we were. If she was at my side, I could live anywhere and have it feel like home.

The realization gripped me tight around the throat. I'd been so dead inside for so many cycles that I hadn't contemplated that the mating bond was just...a confirmation. Trix was already so tightly embedded in my blood that the thought of losing her...

The bike dipped as my hands shook. Trix glanced back in alarm, and she must have seen something on my face, because her eyes went wide. She placed a hand on my arm. "Are you okay?" she shouted over the buzzing of the bikes.

No, no I wasn't flecking okay. What had I been thinking? I'd been so proud of have a strong, smart female at my side that I had agreed to ride into battle with her?

Fleck my life.

TWELVE

Trix

Something was wrong with Kutzal. He'd been fine all morning and then suddenly as we rode over a field of flowers, his body had tensed up. He'd scared the shit out of me, as I thought he'd seen a Joktal or something. But when I'd turned around, his stare was just ... vacant. Deep in thought. And his face had gone pale.

When I'd tried to talk to him, he'd pretty much ignored me. Tired of shouting over the roar of the bikes all around us, I stopped trying to get him to open up. Fine. Whatever. He could sit back there in pale silence. What did I care?

I was going to see my friends soon.

But as the day wore on, Kutzal's silence grew louder. So loud that it drowned out the buzzing of the bikes and all I could hear was his dedication to muteness. But I couldn't ask him about it because we were riding like bats out of hell. The trip would normally take two to three days on foot, and we planned to make it in one day. We'd be there by nightfall, which didn't surprise me as this speed was breakneck. We rode in front with Rex, Mikko, and Fenix while the rest of the warriors flanked us in a triangle. When I looked back, the spectacle of the Drixonian army was nothing short of awesome. I wondered what they'd been like at full strength when their civilization was at its peak. Enemies had to see all the blue skin, thick muscles, dark hair, and piercing violet eyes and want to turn tail and run.

While I was worried that Upreth had bolstered his ranks during the siege, I had to admit that this display of Drixonian power was terrifying. A bunch of aliens on what amounted to flying Harleys? Scary as shit. I was sure glad I'd defected to this side. Team Drix for life.

There wasn't time or energy to deal with Kutzal's mood change. I kept telling myself it was his reaction to the upcoming battle, but I knew Kutzal enough now to know he didn't react like this when faced with a physical challenge. In fact, I think he was relishing the idea of killing a few Joktal. I didn't want to be vain but... did it have to do with me? Was he regretting last night?

I was. At least part of it. The part where I'd gotten angry with him. Maybe I'd let my guard down too much after sex, because when he'd made the comment that insinuated I could get this close to someone else, it had felt like a slap to the face. I knew he didn't mean it that way, and I didn't know when I'd started looking at Kutzal as anything more than a temporary partnership with a common goal.

That morning, I hadn't been able to take my eyes off the loks of the females at Granit. While I'd once seen them as shackles, I now saw them as ... something else. A promise. I had even found myself *envious* of their loks and happy lives. I didn't want a mate ... right? And even if I did, the only Drixonian I'd ever get close to was Kutzal. Since a mate was off-limits for him then ... it was for me too. Why did that cause a sharp pang in my chest?

I shook myself and gritted my teeth as the wind rushed in my face. *Stop it, Trix.* This was the time for focus. I couldn't be distracted around the Joktals, or I was likely to get a clawed club hand right in the guts.

The sun was beginning to drop below the horizon when Kutzal raised his hand in the air and the bikes came to a slow stop at the base of a hill. I gazed up it, detecting a small path leading into dense brush.

I glanced over at Fenix to see him strip off a glove and flex his fingers. The scales of his hand and upper arm were a mass of melted flesh that looked incredibly painful. Snapping his fingers, he nodded with satisfaction as a small flame flickered to life on his palm. With a twist of his wrist, the flame extinguished. His eyes lifted and met mine. Embarrassed to be caught staring, I smiled at him, and he smiled back. "It looks bad, but it doesn't hurt. Not anymore."

There was a relief in his voice that I understood more than he could know. The absence of pain felt like a miracle.

"Should we—" Kutzal began, then stopped suddenly and tilted his head as if listening to something. I held my breath and tried to detect sound through the slight breeze rustling the tall grasses around us but heard nothing.

"Fleck," Rex growled. "Hear that?"

Kutzal's eyes were a little wide as he nodded.

"Hear what?" I asked.

"The siege is over." Kutzal turned on his bike and the others behind us followed suit.

"What do you mean the siege is over?" Panic curled my fingers into my palm. "How do you know?"

"Because the final battle has started." He clenched his jaw. "We got here right on time." He threw his head back.

"*She is All!*" he crowed into the sky. The voices echoing his rose up behind us in a growl of syllables.

We took flight and raced up the hill. I couldn't see much of anything as the bikes spanned out—some riding lower, others higher—in a practiced formation that sent a chill down my spine. We must have ridden a few miles when we crested a hill, and there I got my first look at an alien battle.

A wide, deep ditch surrounded the flat rock of the Drixonian camp. Spikes rested on the ditch bed and the outer rim. While it might have held the Joktals for a few days, they were no longer waiting out the Drixonians. In several places along the ditch, the spikes were nothing but blunt, burnt husks and the Joktals sped across with their charged whips cracking the air.

A solid line of Drixonians blocked their path to the edge of the cliff where a pair of stairs were carved into the rock. I couldn't see below, but Kutzal had explained that they lived in huts on cliff ledges. In the distance, I could make out a rope bridge leading to another cliff with more ledges dotted with small buildings.

The battle was waging, but it was clear the Drixonians had been fighting for a long time... and they were losing. Outnumbered easily five to one, they fought with weapons, machets, and some laser guns. A few rode in the air on their hover bikes, firing at the advancing Joktals, but they couldn't get too close to the whips.

One large Drixonian slashed with two massive broadswords, cleaving a Joktal nearly in two despite his bony armor. But he was bleeding badly from a massive wound in his neck, and he staggered slightly on his big, booted feet. Another hacked away with an ax in a flurry of movement so fast he was nearly a blur. And yet another fought with a grim determination as he slashed with his machets and spiked tail. Most Drixonians were injured, bleeding from blade wounds or whip slashes.

At the sound of our bikes rushing over the hill, they looked up. Two-Sword Drix stabbed at a Joktal before lifting his hand in the air to shade his eyes.

The one with the ax beheaded a Joktal before glaring up at us. "About flecking time, Kutz!"

A familiar whoosh sound flared in my ear, and heat coated the side of my face. A fireball lit into a group of about five Joktals. Their agonized screams as they burst into flames filled the cliff side. The weary Lone Howl Drixonians seemed to feed on the dying cries of their enemies as they fought with renewed vigor.

The Joktals found themselves caged in. Advance to the cliff and meet the Lone Howl, or try to retreat, and they fell to the fresh Drixonian Warriors from Granit. Kutzal sped past a break in the Joktal line to touch his bike down close to the cliff behind the Lone Howl line. The grim-faced warrior with a wicked scar on his face jogged to our side. His eyes went wide at the sight of me, but then quickly focused on his drexel. "Females are—"

"Here!" Tasha's screech was the best sound I'd ever heard in my life. She sped up the cliff stairs carrying a large blade with Amber at her heels.

"I told you to stay hidden—"

His voice cut off as two massive nose hounds raced after them. One was bleeding from its side, likely from Tasha's blade, but the two women were no match for these werewolf-sized fuckers.

"Tash!" The scarred Drix howled her name and leapt toward them, but the nose hounds were going to get there first. I withdrew my bow, notched my arrow, and let it fly. It hit the first nose hound in his throat, and he abruptly reared back with a squeal that sounded like a million demons. I didn't have time to relish my aim. I aimed and fired again, this time at the second nose hound. I hit him in his wound, and the force of the arrow knocked him off his feet. Before either could regain any sort of composure, the scarred Drix was there. With a slash of his machets, he slit their throats, and their bodies shook as the blood drained onto the rock.

Tasha bent over, hands on her knees. "They slipped past your line and found us." She kicked one of the bodies. "They knew our scent."

The scarred Drix reached for her and tugged her against his chest. Her hand wrapped around his biceps and the golden loks on her wrist, which matched his, glittered. "I'm okay." I felt an unfamiliar stab of jealousy and beat it back.

Her eyes found mine and immediately brimmed with tears. "Trix."

"Tasha," I whispered. "Amber."

But there wasn't time for a homecoming. There was a battle going on. Kutzal unsheathed his sword and shot me a look. "Stay here. Shoot any enemy that comes close."

I liked his direct orders and almost saluted him. "Absolutely."

He gave me another look, this one harder to read before he turned and strode toward his fighting warriors.

The scarred warrior raced past me, leaving me standing near Kutzal's bike with Amber and Tasha. They stepped close, not enough to touch, but enough so I could feel their heat. They'd learned just how much I could take.

"Kutzal found you?" Tasha said. I noticed she glanced at my wrists.

"I found him." I kept my bow in front of me, an arrow notched and ready to go.

"This sounds like a story," she mumbled.

"It's a doozy," I laughed and met her gaze for a moment.

Her head was cocked curiously. "He was touching you. You rode in front of him on his bike."

"Yeah, that's another story."

"I've never wanted to hug you as much as I do right now." Amber's curly hair blew in the breeze. A streak of dirt marred her cheek. "I think Vinz can do anything, but even he's tired."

"Vinz is your mate, right? Which one is he?"

She didn't seem surprised I knew. She pointed to the quick one with the ax. Her loks were like a large golden cuff. "There."

A Joktal lifted his whip above Vinz's head, where he stood with his ax held in both hands, chest heaving, back streaked with black blood. I lifted my bow, aimed, and fired it at the Joktal's neck—their weakest spot. The whip fell from his fingers as he staggered back. Vinz froze before slowly turning on his heel. His eyes met mine, and then he shot me a maniacal grin followed by a cackle. After that, he turned and once again entered the battle fray.

"Thank you," Amber whispered.

"I heard one of my arrows was used to shoot him. It's the least I can do."

"But it wasn't you, right?"

"No, but I did shoot Kutzal. On purpose."

"You shot Kutzal?" Tasha cried. "And you're still in one piece?"

"Thank God for *She is All,* right? Or I might be in a ditch somewhere."

"I swear most of them aren't like Kutzal," Tasha's eyes surveyed the battle. "He's the biggest asshole here."

"He's not always an asshole, and when he is, there's usually a reason."

Tasha's eyebrows lifted into her hairline. She blinked at me and then slowly turned to Amber. They had some sort of silent communication, which was pretty damn loud to me.

"Shut up," I grunted at them.

"We didn't say anything," Tasha protested.

"I'll explain. After..." I pointed with another arrow. "This."

Standing in front of my arms, bow raised, I watched the action. Rex circled overhead on his bike as he fired with his laser gun. I had yet to see the appearance of his wings and was only slightly disappointed. Mikko seemed to relish the fighting, hollering as he ejected his wicked black spikes from his arms and back. Those alone took out two Joktals at once. Fenix remained on his bike too as he lobbed fireballs and halted Joktals retreating as he lit trees and foliage on fire.

I searched for Upreth but didn't see him. I would have gone searching for him, but I didn't want to leave Tasha and Amber. Plus, Kutzal had given me an order.

Heart in my throat with worry for him, I searched for him in the crowd and found him fighting next to Two-Sword. They fought back-to-back, swords flashing in the light of the setting sun. Kutzal was fast, strong, and focused. The tip of his sword had great aim, plunging into the few places on the Joktals where they had delicate meaty bits. Still, I jerked every time a Joktal was able to land a blow on his body. Those bunched muscles had been on top of me the other night, for a much different purpose, and I marveled at the way he could be just gentle and kind and yet so very deadly.

Cries of the wounded rang out, and as the Drixonians

pushed the Joktals back and depleted their numbers, Amber, Tasha, and I stalked forward. While the other women tended to the wounded, I kept my bow strung tight in case any Joktals decided to make a break across the Drix line.

Kutzal stepped over the body of the Joktal he just killed and stood with his bloody sword at his side, other first clenched, while he surveyed the waning stages of the battle. Thanks to the three dozen Drix reinforcements, we'd driven the Joktals back. Upreth had definitely come with larger numbers—I would have estimated close to a hundred along with several nose hounds. Two of which lay dead behind us.

The Joktals were retreating. Some made it through the flaming bushes and Drix, but most were cut down in their tracks. Bodies littered the ground of what had once been Kutzal's camp. Several huts on the cliff were nothing but piles of burnt lumber, and I mourned the loss of the home Kutzal had made for his warriors.

Two-Sword laid his hand on Kutzal's shoulder, but the drexel ignored him as he glanced over his shoulder. His eyes found mine. I gave him a solemn nod, a silent, *we did it*, and he returned the gesture.

I dropped my bow, so my arrow pointed at the ground and took a step toward him. I craved a touch from him, even if it was just a slight brush of his fingers. Suddenly his body jerked forward as a crackling snap rent the air.

"Kutzal!" I cried as I began to run.

His body pitched forward, but he caught himself and spun around, sword raised. His back sizzled with vicious whiplash.

Behind him stood the Joktal who'd struck me. *Yirij*. I had long forgotten about him, and I'd assumed he'd perished in the battle, felled by another Drix's sword or machets. But no, of course not. He was here, and he sought to kill Kutzal.

I raised my arrow. "Duck!" I shouted at him. "I have to kill him!" *Me.* Because if Kutzal killed him...

If Kutzal killed him, then he'd get the one thing he didn't want—a bonded mate. A sob wrenched up my throat, and I took a split second to mourn what I'd never have with Kutzal.

"Trix, no!" Came a voice from behind me, and a split second later what felt like a fiery hand wrapped its white-hot fingers around my neck. I let my arrow fly, hoping it found its victim. The fiery band yanked, taking me off my feet. Pain sliced through my body, burning me from the inside out. A blow slammed into the side of my head, and everything went dark.

THIRTEEN

Kutzal

"Trix!" The cry wrenched up my throat like a spiked ball. Out of nowhere, Mikko ran into my vision, his spikes slamming into the eyes of the Joktal whose whip was wrapped around Trix's neck.

I turned onto the Joktal who'd whipped me, knowing he was familiar. Trix had told me once that his name was Yirij. Fatas had saved him for me, and despite what Trix thought, we didn't end here. An arrow stuck out of his shoulder, and he wrenched it out with a snarl.

"Hold him," I barked at Lukent and Axton. "Do *not* kill him. Save him for me."

I didn't wait to watch them follow my orders. I knew they'd get it done. Ignoring the smell of my own burning flesh and the lancing pain cutting into my back, I raced to Trix, sliding onto my knees at her side. Afraid to touch her,

her friends hovered at her side crying and hollering for first aid supplies.

I tugged Trix into my lap, cora in my throat at the red lacerations around her throat. Blood coated the side of her face and slid into her deadly braids. I clenched my jaw to stop myself from howling with rage. Her head lolled, and I placed my hand over her cora. A faint, steady thumping beat against my palm, and a strangled sound left my throat.

"Wake up," I cradled her to my chest. "Please, Trix. You have to wake up, so I can yell at you for what you did."

A water skin was thrust in my face, and I grabbed it. After dripping some over her lips, I poured it over the wounds in her neck. Amber handed me a clean wrap, which I used to dress the wound. With another clean bandage, I swiped at the blood on her face. "Why did you do that?" I murmured softly. Shadows darkened the surrounding ground, and the human females sobbed quietly. "I was going to kill him. I wanted to kill him. And he's still alive so I can show you just how much I want to do this."

When I'd seen his familiar face, I'd felt like it was Fatas confirming a decision I'd already made. No matter what happened in our future, I refused to live it without Trix at my side.

"Kill him," Rex's voice drifted through my distress.

He stood over me, Fenix, and Mikko at his back.

My face must have showed my confusion.

"Killing him will confirm the cora-eternal bond, right?"

I wasn't quite sure how he knew that, but I'd ask later. After I nodded, he gestured to where Axton stood with a foot on the Yirij's back. His two sets of arms were tied tight to his side. "If you kill him, she will heal faster."

"What?" I whispered.

"Sax's mate, Val, would have died if it wasn't for the

power of the loks. It enhances the females in ways we haven't fully explored."

I glanced down at Trix and smoothed loose hair off her damp forehead. She took shallow breaths, and her body hung limp in my arms, which was such a contrast to the strong, controlled Trix I knew.

"If I do, I can't take it back." I swallowed as I glanced at her friends. "She saw the loks as ownership and said she didn't want to be owned again. What if it isn't what she wants?"

Amber buried her face in her hands and sobbed, while Tasha bit her lip as tears streamed down her face. But neither argued with me, which was enough of an answer.

I would do it to save Trix's life. I'd rather have her alive and resent me forever than dead, but the thought of my proud, independent Trix feeling shackled by me curdled my stomach. Clutching her to my chest, I closed my eyes and did the one thing I swore I wouldn't do after watching my family die: I silenty asked Fatas for a favor.

The sounds around me of the crying females and the moans of the wounded fell away, and in its place was the beating of my heart and Trix's shaky breaths. Then a new sound emerged, a rumbling in my chest that surprised me. Instinctively, I was *prushing*. The vibration started slowly before gaining in intensity as prushing was the only way my body knew to comfort the female who was my mate. It was something Drix warriors only did for their mates, and I never thought I'd prush in my life. The soothing vibrations spread throughout my limbs, calming me and causing a hitch in Trix's breathing. I clutched her closer. "Come back to me, please."

Suddenly Trix took a deep gasp and her eyelashes fluttered. A shiver wracked her body, and I propped her up in the crook of my arm as I lightly tapped her cheek.

She inhaled sharply and her eyes opened. Her pupils were blown wide and unfocused. Her lips moved but only a series of dry clicks rattled up her throat.

"Thank Fatas," I whispered.

She swallowed, and her lips moved again. "D-Did I kill him?"

"Don't worry about that."

Her hand flew up and grasped a lock of my hair with urgency. "*Did I?*"

"No," I wrapped my fingers around her forearm. "You didn't."

Her eyes dropped to her wrist, and I might have been imaging things, but I could have sworn I saw disappointment there. "Who did?"

"No one yet," I pointed to where the Yirij lay on his stomach. "But I'm going to, Trix. Do you hear me? I'm going to kill him because I want him dead and because I want what killing him will mean for us."

Her eyes shot to mine. "You do?"

"I'll never see you as just another female I could lose. I'm not a chit anymore. I'm a full-grown warrior. A drexel. And I will fight for a life with you, because that's what I want until Fatas decides to take me." I cupped her cheek. "If you'll have me. I'll never own you. No one will ever own you."

She sniffed as her eyes turned glassy. And when she opened her mouth, she said words that only confirmed she was the perfect mate for me. "Slaughter that motherfucker."

I barked out a laugh as I hauled Trix to her feet. Knowing she'd want her dignity, I made sure she was balanced before I let her go. With her chin proudly jutted in the air, she gave me a stiff nod.

Unsheathing my sword, I walked over to the Joktal. "Untie him and let him up."

Axton made quick work of releasing his bonds. Yirij immediately rolled to his stomach and shuffled away, dirt swirling around his feet. I didn't relish killing another warrior like this, but he'd struck my mate and he'd waged a siege on the only family I knew.

With a vicious upswing of my sword, I speared him under the chin. His eyes went wide as blood dribbled out of his mouth. Tugging out my sword, I let the point rest on the ground while the body of the Joktal fell to the ground in a gurgling heap.

Deed done, I turned back to Trix to find her swaying on her feet. Her friends gripped the loose ends of her clothes to keep her upright, and I admired their ingenuity on how to deal with Trix's inability to be touched.

Dropping my sword to the dirt, I lunged to her side just as she was about to tip over. Her eyes rolled a bit as she tried to focus on me. "Sorry," she mumbled, the word a bit slurred. "Still a bit unsteady."

"Tend to your mate," Lukent said. "You can use our hut. We'll work on cleaning up camp."

I had a lot to tell my warriors, but he was right that my mate was a priority now. "Thank you."

He nodded and turned on a heel to give orders to the standing warriors. I didn't see many wounded Drix, and those that were had injuries similar to mine—whip marks and cuts which would heal.

Suddenly Trix cried out and clutched her hands to her stomach. "What?" I knelt down just as a burning started in my wrists. Although I'd known this would likely be coming, the sight of the black lines appearing on my wrists as if drawn by an invisible hand was still a sight to behold.

"It's the loks," I said to Trix.

"You didn't tell me they hurt," she scowled at me, and that made me smile.

"It's temporary."

But she wasn't scowling anymore. Standing upright without swaying with her hands held in front of her, she rotated her wrists back and forth as the loks completed. The two lines with a design inside glowed a bright white before fading to a light gold.

Trix

As I stared at the loks on my wrists, my heart pounded and sweat broke out on my temples. When Kutzal had first told me about the loks, I'd imagined they'd feel stifling. I thought I'd be trapped.

But instead, the emotion surging through me was wholly new. A warmth that coated me inside out like a protective shield. The ache in my chest that had been present since I'd learned about my aversion to touch was no longer there. And as my eyes met Kutzal, I realized that the ache had been loneliness. Even surrounded by my girls, the absence of physical touch had burrowed itself deep inside like a splinter.

That splinter was gone, the bleeding was stemmed, and for the first time in a long time, I felt contentment.

Kutzal lurched toward me on unsteady feet. He gripped my face with gentle hands. "Trix? Are you okay?"

A swirl of golden smoke warped and shifted in my mind. When I reached up and wrapped a hand around Kutzal's wrists, the smoke settled as if expectant. "I'm okay. Are you?" I had to know if he was regretting the decisions to kill Yirij himself.

His eyes softened. "I'm okay. I'm good."

"Really?"

He smiled then. "Really."

"We're—" I swallowed. "We're bonded now, right?"

His thumbs swiped under my eyes. "We are, but it feels like a formality. I didn't want to admit it at the time, but I was gone for you the moment you shot me."

I snorted. "You lie."

He shook his head. "No, I don't." The golden smoke shivered as if pleased. I tapped my temple. "Why is there... something in here that seems to mimic your emotions."

"We call it your aura," Amber stepped closer to our sides. "You can feel his emotions and he can feel yours."

I marveled at that. "He's like golden smoke."

"And you're a windstorm holding me together."

I lifted a hand to my neck. "And I feel okay. A little pain but I no longer want to throw up."

He dropped his hands from my face and wrapped an arm around my shoulders. "Still, you need to rest."

"But we need to tell—"

"I know," he cut me off. "Leave that to me. Go spend time with Amber and Tasha, rest, and eat."

Nearby, some of the Granit warriors were already digging through the supplies and handing them out to members of the Lone Howl clavas. Fenix handed Amber a large parcel with a smile. "Some cured meats, breads, and fruits from the females at Granit. I think they made a few treats too."

"Thank you," Amber said, her eyes greedily taking in the package.

"How were you with food and supplies while under siege?" I asked.

"We didn't starve." Tasha stepped to my side. "But if I have to eat another handful of bland nuts, I might lose my mind."

"Let me check to make sure the huts are clear," said the scarred warrior as he walked ahead of us.

"I'm coming too." Vinz wrapped his arm around Amber's shoulders and pressed a kiss to her temple. He was covered in blood and dirt but still seemed to have boundless energy and nearly bounced on his toes as he walked.

Kutzal squeezed my hand and let me go. "I'll find you after I deal with the aftermath."

As much as I didn't want to let him go, I was exhausted, hungry, and dying of thirst. Most of all, I very much wanted to talk to my friends. Tasha walked at my side as we descended the stone stairs of the cliff. She pointed to the scarred warrior who talked ahead of us, searching each hut before he deemed it safe. "That's Lukent, my mate. I call him Kent."

"I heard he saved you from the Wutarks."

"And just in time. They were about to launch me off a cliff and I would have been nothing but a Tasha pancake."

I shuddered. "Don't say that."

"It's the truth."

"And he's... good to you?"

She eyed me. "You know the answer to that."

I did, but I needed her to confirm it for my own peace of mind. "Just answer the question."

"Of course, he is," she said softly, her gaze finding him immediately. "He's sweet and gentle despite the fierce way he fights. But Kutzal is the last one I thought would be mated. I'm sure it's a story, right?"

I laughed. "Oh boy, is it."

She grinned. "I can't wait to hear it."

After all the huts were searched, Amber, Tasha, and I settled into an empty one. I lounged at the head of the bed pallet, Amber rested at the foot crosswise, and Tasha sat on the floor as she opened the parcel of food.

Groaning, she held up a loaf of something that looked a lot like banana bread and smelled like it too. "I could eat this entire thing myself."

"You two take that." I reached for a wedge of cheese and thin slices of a cured meat. "I was just at Granit and had a good meal."

Tasha paused while handing Amber a slice of the bread. "You were at Granit?"

"Eat," I urged. "And I'll explain."

Amber and Tasha didn't need to be told twice. They stuffed their mouths with an assortment of food while I started from the beginning—how I'd been tricked by the Joktals, helped them capture Kutzal, and then I'd learned the truth. I skipped some of the details about his past because that wasn't my story to tell.

"Kutzal let me know that you two were mated but forgot to tell me that there was a whole damn colony of human and Drixonian mates at Granit. I woke up to see a woman named Val and nearly passed out."

Tasha smiled. "Val is sweet."

"I had to trust Kutzal, because my gut told me too and because I didn't know what else to do. But finding them there, and Val telling me she'd met you, really helped put my mind at ease."

"Okay but... Kutzal?" Amber asked around a mouthful of bread. "How can he touch you?"

"My alter has never been very consistent. Sometimes I can be touched briefly; you both know that. But with Kutzal, I don't know what happened. It started out that I didn't have pain as long as I touched him first, and then it evolved into..." I waved a hand. "This. Touching. No pain. I don't get it either."

"Is your pain gone?" Tasha asked.

"No, I don't think so. Val tried to touch me to treat me, and the pain was nearly unbearable." I swallowed and held out my hand. "Here, touch me."

Tasha's lips pulled into a grimace. "But—"

"Just try. Lightly. I'll pull away when it starts to hurt."

Swallowing, she hesitantly placed the tips of her fingers on my wrist. At first, I felt nothing, and my heart soared, but then the familiar burn began, and I yanked my hand away with a frustrated growl. "Well, there's the answer."

"Shit, I was hoping he was the cure or something."

I shook my head. "I don't think there is a cure. Are you two still affected by your mods? Tasha, how are your nosebleeds? Amber, do you need to sleep as often?"

Tasha tapped her nose. "I still get them. You should have seen Lukent's face the first time I got one. We couldn't communicate yet because our implants weren't updated, and I was still iffy on whether he wanted to eat me. But his concern over my bloody nose was unmistakable. Later, he told me he thought I was going to die."

"And I still fall into a deep sleep every few days. Like Tasha, I thought Vinz might want to eat me but when I stayed up too long and passed out, he protected me from the Joktals."

My heart lurched. "I know how you hate being so vulnerable when you sleep."

She smiled. "He gets it."

Tasha's hand found hers on the bed, and they laced their fingers together. I wished I could join them, and maybe one day I could. For now, with my belly full, all I wanted to do was sleep.

"You should clean your wound before you rest," Tasha urged.

In my excitement to eat and talk to Tasha and Amber, I'd been ignoring my aches and pains. I reached up to prod at the wrap around my neck. The skin felt raw and tender underneath. "Not looking forward to seeing this."

Tasha bit her lip, which told me it was as bad as it felt. She showed me the attached cleanser, and I ditched my clothes to stand underneath the filtered air. When I turned off the cleanser, Amber stood outside with a fresh set of clothes. They helped me bandage my head and wrap my neck, which was healing surprisingly fast. Tasha explained that the cora-eternal bond gave us humans some faster healing abilities like the Drixonians, which blew my mind.

I lay down, but as tired as I was, I couldn't seem to fall asleep. My head still felt full, and the golden smoke of Kutzal's aura was active. I would have to get used to that.

"Do we know anything about Lu, Maisie, and Neve?" I asked.

Tasha stretched out on a fur beside the bed with her hands folded behind her head. Amber curled up next to her on her side. "Not yet." Tasha played with Amber's curls. "Kutzal promised to help look for them, and many of the warriors have been, but the damn Joktals and Wutarks keep interrupting us."

"Shit," I grumbled. "Of all the girls to still be missing..."

My sentence hung in the air around us, and I didn't need to finish it. Tasha and I had been the leaders with Amber a strong third. Lu and Maisie were like our bratty younger sisters who we loved anyway. And Neve was ... a wild card. She didn't talk much and didn't appear to have an altar. But she was overwhelmingly kind, caring, and patient with all of us. She would always be the first to help if someone got hurt and never complained no matter how tired she was.

"Fuck." I rubbed my face. "We'll speak to Daz. I bet he'll help."

"Is he coming here?" Tasha tilted her head to meet my gaze.

I shifted to the edge of the bed pallet to break the news to her. "No, Tash. We're going there."

"Where?" she frowned.

"Granit. Well, not Granit, but a village nearby."

She sat up, dislodging Amber who let out a grunt of protest. "What? We're leaving here after defending it?"

"You defended *people*. Beings. Not a place."

Tasha's eyes darkened. I knew she wouldn't like this news. She'd made this her home, and I couldn't blame her for not wanting to move again.

"That was the condition for Daz to send warriors to help end the siege. He said we had to move closer so we could be a part of the Drixonian community."

A muscle in Tasha's jaw ticked. "Does he want them closer so it's easier to send the sons of naught off on the dangerous missions?"

"Tash," I said softly. "You met him. Did he give you that impression?"

With her arms crossed over her chest and her chin jutted out, she looked like a petulant child. "No."

"I get where you're coming from. When Kutzal told me how he and the others had been treated, I hadn't wanted anything to do with other Drixonians. But Daz made a pretty significant impression. He told Kutzal that he and the rest of this clavas are important, and not just because they have mated females. He's abolishing the sons of naught condition. No more branding. No more shunning. Nothing."

Tasha's expression softened and she glanced down at her lap. "That actually does sound like him."

"I know it's only been the six of us for so long, but the women at Granit are kind and thoughtful."

"They are." Tasha said to Amber. "You'll like them."

Amber smoothed her hand over the fur blanket. "I always felt like Lu and Maisie would benefit from a larger community."

"I know it'll be an adjustment, but Daz said he'd prepare a small village for us. So, we'll be near Granit but not ... in it."

"That's a good idea," Tasha said. "I'm not sure many of these warriors will love a crowd."

"Can you imagine Axton around a bunch of Drix babies?" Amber snorted.

"Who's Axton?" I asked. "Kutzal mentioned him once or twice."

"He's the biggest of the Lone Howl warriors. He doesn't say much but fights with two swords like a beast. When not fighting he's sleeping or eating. And he definitely does not enjoy a lot of talking around him."

I made a face. "So, keep him away from Lu when we find her."

Tasha laughed. "That's maybe a good idea."

With a smile on my face, my eyelids felt heavy. While

we still had more work to do, we now had half of our group, and that was better than we'd had yesterday. I yawned and Tasha did the same a moment later.

"Sleep," Amber said with her head on Tasha's chest. "I'm good for another day or so."

She didn't have to tell me twice. My eyes closed, and I was out a moment later.

FOURTEEN

Kutzal

"We have to *what*?" Vinz's screech hurt my ears.

I glared at him. "You heard me the first time. You just want to be dramatic."

"Actually, no, I'm pretty sure I heard you wrong," Vinz sassed me.

Axton opened his eyes long enough to cuff him on the back of the head. "Knock it off."

"Did you hear him?" Vinz whirled around to face Axton. "I thought you were asleep."

"You know he hears shet even when he's sleeping." Lukent then ignored Vinz and focused on me. "This condition is non-negotiable?"

"Non-negotiable," I answered. "And in fact, I don't want to negotiate it. Daz is right. If we're closer to Granit, we'll be able to defend ourselves better. It's good for our females and eventually..." I swallowed. "Our families. When I decided this was the best place for us, I never imagined we'd possibly have females heavy with our chits walking around the cliffs. What if we had a siege again?"

Vinz stiffened. "They were never in danger."

"I understand that. But chits aren't meant for siege life." I fisted my hands and went in for the kill. "I want better for them than what we had, Vinz."

That remark hit its target. Vinz visibly flinched and then fell silent. We stood around the remnants of my hut. The sun had risen a little while ago, shedding light on the carnage that had occurred overnight. The camp was littered with Joktal bodies and several wounded Drix lay grouped together while our healers tended to them. We had no casualties, and only one of the injuries seemed life-threatening. The uninjured Lone Howl and Granit warriors piled up the bodies to prepare to burn them.

My one regret is that we didn't find Upreth. He'd escaped, likely with his closest warriors. But at least we'd shown them our strength.

The sight of the home I'd made with my warriors now in disrepair felt like a jagged stone in my gut. The hut where I'd held countless meetings and got buzzed on Xavy's spirits and our yuza plant was nothing but a burnt husk.

This home had served us well, but it was time to move on. Eyes half closed and his arms crossed, Axton leaned on what was left of my back wall. Blood dripped from his elbow, but I knew it wasn't his.

Lukent stood with his hands on his hips, jaw tight. Of all my closest friends, I knew he'd come to the conclusion that this was the best decision first. My assumption proved right when he lifted his head with a resolute gaze. "Let's give the wounded another rotation to heal and we'll pack up. The Granit warriors will travel back with us?" When I nodded in answer, he dropped his hands. "I'm going to get Tasha and spend one last night in our hut."

Vinz pushed at a blackened pole that had once been a chair leg. "I'll get Amber. She'll want to sleep before we leave."

"Tomorrow at sunup, we'll leave," I said to their backs as they walked away. Vinz ignored me, but Lukent waved a hand over his shoulder.

Axton hadn't moved. I nudged his shoulder, and he cracked an eye open. "What?"

"Anything to say?"

He fully opened his eyes and tapped a finger on his forearm. "It's the right call. Daz is wise to suggest it, and you're wise to accept it."

"I'm glad you think so." I turned to walk away.

"I won't be staying long though."

That got my attention. I turned on my heel. "What?"

His eyes were a darker violet than I'd ever seen in a Drixonian. "I'm going to look for the other females."

"I'm going to talk to Daz—"

"And that's fine. But I want to try on my own now that I know the Lone Howl is safer closer to Granit."

"It's not only your duty."

"Maybe, but I'm good at what I do." He snorted. "The Granit warriors can fight, but can they track? They might have lost their edge in that fancy city."

"Don't let them hear you say that."

Using muscles he rarely bothered with, Axton grinned. "I'll be good."

"Get some rest. I'm going to check on Trix."

"Will do, drexel."

I found Trix asleep in one of our less-used huts. I would have loved to see her among my furs in my own hut, but they were nothing but ash now. I hadn't had many belongings. In fact, the only possession I cared about was the bracelet currently on Trix's wrist.

I used the expeller and walked out naked. Fatigue was beginning to set into my bones. Anxiousness had simmered under my skin for many rotations on a slow boil and had only cooled now once I knew those I cared about were safe.

I'd feel better once we settled in our new village. Travel would be slow as we'd be weighted down with supplies and injured warriors, but at least we had three dozen Drix riding with us.

A plate of half-eaten food sat on a table, and I dropped most of it in my mouth, swallowing without chewing.

When I lay down next to Trix, her breathing hitched, and her eyes opened blearily. I tucked a stray lock of auburn hair behind her ear. "Go back to sleep."

But of course she didn't listen to me. Her gaze slid down my chest to where the fur blanket covered my groin. Resting a hand on my arm, she smiled. "You're clean."

I briefly touched my nose to hers. "So are you." I inspected the gash on her head, which had already begun to scab over. The whip wound on her neck was still tender, but it would heal.

Her fingers touched her throat. "It'll scar."

I drew her hand away and laced our fingers together. "When that whip wrapped around your neck, I thought I'd die. Truly. A scar doesn't matter. You being alive matters."

"I know, I'm not that vain." She squeezed my fingers. "What happened when I was passed out?"

"Rex told me to kill Yirij because the cora-eternal bond could save you. Val would have died without it. As much as

I wanted to save you, I also didn't want to bond you to me without asking you first. So, then you opened your eyes and gave me the command. I didn't look back."

"And you wanted it?"

I cupped her cheek. "Trix, I realized something on the way here."

"I knew you were acting weird."

"Because I had to work some things out in my head. But the truth was that I didn't see you as a burden on my cora. I was a chit when my family died, but I'm not a chit anymore. I will fight for this future with you. I've battled for it this far. I intend to do it until I take my last breath." I held her gaze, so she felt my sincerity. "I want a future with you at my side."

Her eyes watered. "I want it too." She sniffed. "When we left Granit, I found I was actually jealous of the females with their loks and mates. I never thought I'd feel that way."

I pressed a kiss to the inside of her wrist, over her loks. The pattern inside resembled wispy swirls of smoke.

She smiled. "And being nice to you doesn't make me want to hurl anymore."

"Oh, how far we've come," I murmured. Her lips pressed to mine, and I drank her down, tasting the freshness of the qua on her breath and the saltiness of the cheese she'd eaten. I rolled on top of her and caged her in with my arms. She stared up at me with flushed cheeks and swollen lips. "I should be making plans. We leave tomorrow at sunup."

"No, you should be making me come." Her fingernails scratched down my ribs, and a shiver snaked down my spine.

I groaned as the windstorm of her aura kicked up a notch in my mind. The winds swirled around, tempting me with flashes of lightning.

"You're a seductress." I growled.

As her wicked tongue probed the corner of her lips with a cheeky grin, her thin fingers grasped my cock and squeezed. I groaned and bucked into her hand. I hadn't realized she wasn't wearing much either—only an oversized shirt and a thin pair of underclothes.

"Take these clothes off," I grunted.

She made quick work on getting as naked as I was, and I slipped down her body to settle myself between her legs. Trix's green eyes glowed in the morning light, and when I placed my mouth on her clit, she cried out. As much as I wanted to draw this out, my cock ached and Trix's cries of pleasure spurred me on. I wanted to see her fall apart. Plunging two fingers inside of her slick cunt, I worked that pleasure bud with my tongue and my lips until she came on a shuddering cry.

Crawling up her body, I slid into her cunt in one smooth motion. Her hands flailed as she arched her back. "Come again on my cock, mate," I grunted as I slammed into her. My subcock extended and latched onto her already slick clit. "You're soaked from my tongue, but now I want you soaking my cock."

"Oh God," she moaned as she writhed beneath me. I pounded into her hard, one hand braced above her head while I dug my knees into the bed for purchase. Beneath me, she went wild, fighting me like any good prey. I took a fingernail to the chin and licked at the blood there. Trix bared her teeth as her inner walls rippled around me. Sucking in a breath, she let out a loud moan as her body shuddered. Her windstorm wracked the walls of my mind. The sight of her reaching her climax was all I needed. Shouting my release, I came inside my mate with every muscle tensed.

When my body went slack, I gathered Trix in my arms and rolled us to our sides. I panted while the hard buds of her nipples rubbed against my chest. With her face tucked into my neck, she dropped tiny kisses on my scales there. "I love you Kutzal," she whispered.

I'd heard Tasha say the words to Lukent. I knew what they meant, and I knew the words were a very big deal to the human females. "I love you too, Trix."

"Do you know what it means?" She settled on her back, skin flushed a pretty pink.

I ran a finger over her beaded nipples, and she huffed out a laugh before swatting my hand away.

"I think Tasha said it to Lukent. It means declaring your dedication to someone else, right?"

"Sure, that's a definition that works." She settled her hand over where my cora was still racing. "Different people think it means different things. When I say it, it means that I'm committed to you, and I want a happy future with you as your mate."

"That's what I mean but also..." I placed my hand over hers. "My cora beats for you."

She smiled and nuzzled into my chest. "And mine for you."

———

My skin prickled as I stared out over the remains of our camp. We'd cleaned up what was left of our fire pit and the burned buildings. The huts that we'd built we left standing. Maybe another species—hopefully less-hostile ones—would be able to make this their home in the future. If not, we wanted it habitable in case we ever had to return.

The rope bridge connected to the two cliffs where we made our home swayed in the gentle morning breeze.

Trix stood beside me with her hair neatly plaited and her bow and arrows strapped to her back. The Lone Howl warriors flanked behind me while the Granit warriors had already descended the hill and waited for us there with their hover bikes and the sleds of supplies.

They'd given us the time to say goodbye to this place where we'd once settled with a resigned duty. On my other side, Axton stood with his hair swirling around his shoulders and his twin swords strapped to his back.

"We've moved on from what we wanted to accomplish when we settled here," he murmured softly.

Surprised he'd said anything, let alone something deep, I cast him a glance. He continued to stare out at our camp until finally his head turned. With a pat on my shoulder, his dark eyes creased at the corners. "You led us to a brighter future than most of us could have hoped for."

"Even you?" I queried.

Axton was a warrior through and through—he obeyed orders and rarely showed initiative, which was why I had been so surprised at his declaration to search for the females on his own.

"Even me," he replied.

After another pat on my arm, he turned and walked down the hill. Loaded with supplies on their backs, the other warriors followed, until only Trix and I remained. Her hand slid into mine. "We can come back and visit if you'd like."

I shook my head. "No, this is my past now."

She must have read something in my face, or in my aura, because she fell silent.

"I lived for them, my warriors, for all these cycles," I

said. "And that made me content enough. It had been so long since I'd seen my mother and my sisters that I hadn't remembered what it was like to be happy." I lifted our hands and pressed a kiss to her knuckles. "And now that I remember, I'm not letting it go."

Her tongue peeked out from between her lips as she grinned. "Who knew you were so good with sappy words?"

"Don't tell the warriors," I grunted. "I have a reputation to uphold."

"Oh, I'm pretty sure they've seen the sap now. You can't take it back."

"Maybe we should stage a fight."

Her eyes lit up as I tugged her down the hill at my side. "*Ooo*, a fight! Yeah, let's do it. Can I shoot you?"

"No."

"Well, we have to make it real."

"I was joking. Do you have to be so excited to shoot me?"

She stuck her lip out. "I wasn't going to actually shoot you. Just... get really close."

I narrowed my eyes at her. "No."

"Fine. So, what can we fight about?"

"I wasn't serious about fighting."

She seemed to deflate, then she perked up again. "We're kind of fighting now."

Careful of the still heating cut on her head. I swung my arm around the back of her neck and tucked her head into my side. She let out a yelp and then a cackling laugh. "Get off me!"

"No."

"Quit saying no!"

"Quit fighting with me."

Half-running, half-fighting, we made it to the bottom of

the hill to find three dozen warriors plus my Lone Howl clavas staring at us in silence. I immediately let Trix go and cleared my throat. But she didn't get the clue. With a weird rally cry, she kneed me in the back of my leg. My knee buckled and she shouted in triumph as I stumbled to the side and shot her a vicious look.

Instead, she put her fists up near her face. "Come at me!"

"Trix," I hissed with a head jerk to show our audience. "Stop it."

Her eyes slid to the side, and she went very still. Then she coughed a few times into her fists and faced them with a casual stance. "Hello, everyone. Just, uh, sparring. We like to do that. Keeps us fresh, you know?"

She shadow-boxed the air.

Tasha let out an amused snort. "That's nice. Are you two done now? Can we leave?"

Trix bit her lip and turned to me with a wince. "*Sorry*," she mouthed.

I held back a laugh. "Tell 'em."

"What?"

"Tell 'em we're ready to go."

Her mouth opened in unparalleled glee. With a fist in the air, she hollered at the top of her lungs. "Let's ride!"

The air filled with the whoops of Drixonian warriors, the buzz of hover bikes, and the delighted laughter of human females.

EPILOGUE

Trix

The trip to the village outside Granit took over two days. We'd flown there like bats out of hell to fight the siege, but this time, surrounded by so many warriors and loaded with supplies, the travel took longer. Not that anyone really complained. Overall, the mood was upbeat, optimistic even. Fenix started a fire for us every night, and the stolen warriors told stories around the campfires.

I was a little ashamed I'd thought some of the females at Granit were pampered. Mikko had met Ryan in a prison pit full of nasty beasties and they'd barely escaped with their lives. Tasha had met and talked with Mikko's mate, Ryan, when she'd visited Granit and was eager to see her again.

The stolen warriors directed us to the village, as it had been their home before they'd moved to Granit. The village was surrounded by woods and plenty of game, according to Rex, and we rode into the center of the village where a large moke tree took up the center. Quaint benches surrounded the thick trunk, and there were humble cabins lining a wide dirt path.

A vine decoration hung from the tree twisted to spell out the word *Welcome*. The sight of it made a lump grow in my throat. Amber went ahead and cried tears of joy while Tasha leapt off Vinz's bike and twirled in a circle.

Rex approached where Kutzal and I still sat on his bike. "Name the village whatever you like. It's your home permanently now. Make it yours."

"Thank you," Kutzal said. "For all you've done."

"We're going to leave you to it. I can see our females were busy, and I believe they left you a cooked meal in the dining hut. I'm eager to see my mate, so we'll be riding back to Granit."

Kutzal took the time to walk around to all the Granit warriors, thanking them in turn for helping. He spoke longer to the few who were injured, although most expressed that they were happy to participate.

As the Granit warriors left, Kutzal and I explored. Our arms brushing, we walked through the center of the village while most of the Lone Howl warriors strode around, throwing open doors and shouting to each other like kids at their first beach house.

Axton claimed a cabin at the far outskirts of the village. He told us it was for protection purposes so he could observe the border, but Kutzal whispered to me that he just wanted his alone time. Lukent and Vinz settled on cabins near the largest one, which Kutzal claimed for us.

Food smells emanated from the dining hut, a large open-air pavilion scattered with tables. A fire pit and other cooking supplies lined one side. The Lone Howl warriors descended on the food, but I was too excited to eat. Kutzal and I hovered near the entrance of the dining hut to watch the warriors eat.

"So, what will you name the village?" I asked.

"I don't know," he answered thoughtfully.

I gripped his hand. "What was your mother's name?"

He startled, and his eyes swung to me. "My mother?"

"Yeah."

His throat bobbed as he swallowed. "Sari."

"That's a pretty name. What if we name the village Sari after your mother?"

He stared at me a long while with his expression unreadable. His aura was rather still, so I couldn't make out if I'd upset him or not. Finally, his lips spread into a sad smile. "I'd like that."

My heart lightened. "Yeah?"

Sticking his fingers in his mouth, he let out a piercing whistle. The crowd of warriors fell silent, some pausing with their utensils halfway to their mouths. "Keep eating," Kutzal spoke over the crowd. "I have a few things to say. I want to first thank you all for making the journey here and trusting me to have your best interests in mind. I am proud to be your drexel, and I'll always do my best to keep you safe."

Many of the warriors crossed their arms at the wrist in front of their necks and murmurs of "*She is All*" rippled over the crowd.

Kutzal nodded. "This village is ours. And I've chosen to name it Sari, after my mother."

The *She is All* chants grew louder and booted feet stomped the ground. Green dirt swirled under the tables. Soon, the chant morphed into another word. *Sari.*

"*Sari, Sari, Sari, Sari.*"

The chant filled the air, and Kutzal's golden smoke aura

lifted into the air and swelled until my entire mind felt full of glitter.

Seated with their mates, Tasha and Amber banged their fists on the tables, mouths wide with laughter, as they chanted along.

"Sari, Sari, Sari, Sari."

My voice joined the chant. Kutzal clasped my hand and lifted it in the air. When his deep voice finally boomed the chant as well, I knew that we'd finally found our home.

Thank you so much for reading The Alien's Battle! I'd appreciate it if you drop me a rating and review on Amazon and Goodreads!

If you're new to my books, please check out my website for my bibliography and reading order, www.ellamaven.com

What's next? Axton and Lu's story in
THE ALIEN'S BOUNTY.

She's something I didn't want, but everything I crave.

Lu: This planet is the pits. I'm being handed off to different aliens one after another like I'm a dog-eared novel. My latest captors are about to take me off planet when a big blue alien botches the rescue mission. Now we're both prisoners of a fierce lizard species who will let us free on one condition, and I think our life span is looking bleak.

Axton: I know my way around swords, enemies, and blood, but this human is something else. She never stops talking, asks too many questions, and makes my blood hot. All we need to do is find the missing offspring of the lizard king. Between my muscles and her sporadic ability to tell the future, I figure we might just make it out alive.

While battling for our lives, I'm also fighting to keep my hands off the fiery human. But time is running out, and if I want a future with her, I have to complete the hardest hunt of my life.

ABOUT THE AUTHOR

Ella Maven is the pen name for a multi-published USA Today Bestselling author who decided to finally unleash the alien world that had been living in her head for years. (Is that weird? Probably). Her books feature dominant, possessive aliens who are absolutely devoted to their humans.

She lives on the East Coast with her completely normal husband and two spawn who sure seem alien some days.

ALSO BY ELLA MAVEN

The Alien's Sacrifice

The Alien's Surrender

Standalones:

Claimed by the Demon Alien

Made in the USA
Las Vegas, NV
29 November 2024

12886409R00104